Readers love the
A Sucker for Love Mysteries
by K.L. HIERS

Acsquidentally In Love

"This book has a bit of everything I love, a good mystery, magic, romance, humor, and Action. K.L. Hiers has me hooked and I can't wait for more!"

—Bayou Book Junkie

"Hiers rolls worldbuilding mythology, delicious flirting, erotic scenes, and detective work into a breezy and sensual LGBTQ paranormal romance."

—Library Journal

Kraken My Heart

"I am so in love with this series... This is a really good series. It is one that is worth reading over again, just for the fun of it."

—Love Bytes Reviews

By K.L. Hiers

A SUCKER FOR LOVE
Acsquidentally In Love
Kraken My Heart
Head Over Tentacles
Nautilus Than Perfect

Published by Dreamspinner Press
www.dreamspinnerpress.com

Nautilus Than Perfect

K.L. Hiers

DREAMSPINNER
PRESS

Published by
DREAMSPINNER PRESS

5032 Capital Circle SW, Suite 2, PMB# 279, Tallahassee, FL 32305-7886 USA
www.dreamspinnerpress.com

Nautilus Than Perfect
© 2021 K.L. Hiers

Cover Art
© 2021 Tiferet Design
http://www.tiferetdesign.com

Trade Paperback ISBN: 978-1-64108-291-4
Digital ISBN: 978-1-64108-290-7
Trade Paperback published October 2021
First Edition
v. 1.0

Printed in the United States of America
⊗
This paper meets the requirements of
ANSI/NISO Z39.48-1992 (Permanence of Paper).

CHAPTER 1.

"GOOD MORNING," Detective Benjamin Merrick greeted, sitting down at his desk across from Chase's inside the war room of the Archersville Police Department. "I already checked with forensics about the residue from our stolen crystal shipment. Still no match. I reviewed our reports for the Lunderson case and turned them in to Captain Quinn. Oh, and I also spoke to the medical examiner about Mr. Destiny Unknown, and his identity remains unknown." He paused. "How are you?"

Detective Elwood Q. Chase made a small grunting sound. He was recovering from a hangover and was in no mood for Merrick's go-getter attitude so early in the morning.

Merrick could have walked right onto a movie set with his perfect suit and his stupid perfect face. Chase was rumpled and wrinkled, and the five o'clock shadow he'd neglected for weeks was now a full beard.

It was obvious that they would never see eye to eye on grooming habits, nor would they ever agree on what an appropriate time was for having to be so miserably awake.

"Here," Merrick said, his voice suddenly dropping to a whisper as he slid something across his desk to Chase's. "While I was heading back from forensics, I secured the last cream-filled eclair for you before Daisy could get it."

"You're a god amongst men." Chase accepted the pastry and took a big bite.

"Just looking out for my partner," Merrick said with an affectionate eye roll. "Besides, staff are encouraged to only take one pastry, and she was already on her third." He cleared his throat. "She very clearly *donut* understand the rules." He beamed at Chase expectantly.

"Yup. Got it." Chase gave a thumbs-up.

Merrick frowned, looking over Chase more intently. "You look unwell. Rough night?"

"Mmm." Chase grunted again, and he shoved the rest of the eclair in his mouth to avoid answering. He'd stayed up too late in the intimate company of a box of wine and passed out before he could use a sobering spell. He wasn't in the mood for jokes.

"Well," Merrick went on without missing a beat, "we have received reports of trespassing at the old Lieben factory, and we must investigate them."

"Mmm."

"I'll drive."

"Mmhm."

"Are you ready?"

"Almost." Chase licked an errant bit of icing off his fingers. "Lieben factory. What's that? One of the old shoe places?"

"You would know this if you had actually attended the briefing this morning," Merrick scolded.

"I was working extra hard on my beauty sleep." Chase gestured to his face. "You can't rush a stunning vision like this. It takes time."

"Uh-huh." Merrick, as usual, was not amused.

Chase had learned some time ago that Merrick only laughed at the corniest of jokes and puns. It was endearing and equally annoying.

"Trust me. You should laugh at that one. It's hilarious." Chase staggered to his feet, checking the gun at his hip and the silencing flare next to it. He put his jacket on and reached for his hat, an old brown fedora. "Okay, Merry. Let's fuckin' go."

"Wait, hold still," Merrick said, reaching up to gently brush at Chase's beard around his mouth. "The eclair does not need to come with us."

Freezing in place, Chase gawked at Merrick as his fingers touched his cheek. His pulse picked up, and a swarm of butterflies promptly invaded his gut. He should push him away, stop him from being so invasive, but he didn't want to.

It took all of Chase's willpower not to stare at Merrick's lips. It wasn't often they were this close, and he didn't want to be a lech. He said a silent prayer to the Lord of Light or Azaethoth or whoever was up there to let this moment last a little longer.

Merrick pulled away all too quickly. His face was unreadable, apparently not as affected as Chase was. "There. Now you look presentable."

"Hey," Chase scolded, unable to stop himself from grinning, "you don't know that I wasn't just saving that for later."

"Hmmph."

"Next time I'll make sure to get it on my pants."

"You know fraternization is strongly frowned upon, Detective Chase. I do not like what you are implying."

"You *donut* like anything," Chase teased.

The tiniest smile cracked Merrick's stoic stare. "I like catching criminals. Let us go."

"You're no fuckin' fun."

"That kind of language is unwelcome and violates the code of conduct for how an officer of the law should speak."

"Eat a dick, Merrick." Chase slid his hat on and tipped it. "How's that for unwelcome?"

"Cute. I am still driving."

Fuck, being in love with such a jerk was tough.

It was hard to pinpoint exactly when Chase had fallen for Merrick. As they drove over to the factory, he found himself staring out the window and trying to remember how he'd gotten into this mess.

Took some time, he knew that. Despite their differences, they had managed to find a solid balance as partners over the years. What started as bickering and resentment soon turned into cracking cases and arresting criminals left and right. Chase helped temper Merrick's poor personal skills, and Merrick made Chase strive to be a better cop.

Maybe even a better person, though he didn't think he had enough years left to catch up, being at least fifteen years Merrick's senior. Merrick's relentless determination and drive for justice was like a light, and Chase couldn't get enough of it. He'd never met anyone as brave or courageous as Merrick, and he was in constant awe of him.

The best Chase felt like he could do was try not to hold Merrick back and bask in his beautiful fire.

And maybe get him to laugh on occasion.

That was nice.

More than that? Just wasn't meant to be.

He'd never known Merrick to date before, didn't even know what he liked, but it definitely wasn't Chase. Chase was old, pasty and freckled, fat, his once deep red hair turning blond now, and every day he found a new crease beneath his eyes. Merrick was young, athletic, black, with gorgeous dark skin and the bluest eyes Chase had ever seen. There was no way in hell he'd give an old slob like Chase a try.

Not in a million years.

He wasn't about to set himself up for rejection when he already knew what the outcome would be. There was maybe this one time he'd drunk dialed Merrick and asked him to come over. When Merrick asked what the nature of the visit would be, Chase had told him it was personal.

He'd said a bunch of other stupid things, though most of it was a drunken blur. He had definitely told him clothing would be optional and recalled Merrick promptly hanging up on him after that.

Not his proudest moment, but that had been months ago, and Merrick was polite enough to never mention it.

Chase was grateful and had resigned himself to admiring Merrick in secret. What they had as partners now wasn't worth screwing up with his stupid feelings, no matter what some crazy love goddess said.

The love goddess....

There was something about that day he kept trying to remember, a piece of something lost he couldn't get back. His head was already hurting from his hangover, and trying to think about it made it worse. He didn't remember ever having headaches like this before, but he'd been drinking a bit more than usual.

He'd managed to lose his own damn badge a few weeks ago, and he had no idea what the hell happened to it. Its location was lost somewhere up in his brain with whoever that love goddess was.

Fuck it.

"You okay?" Merrick asked suddenly, breaking into Chase's thoughts.

"Mmm, yeah. I'm good." Chase shifted in his seat. "So, tell me what I missed in the briefing. What's up with this factory?"

"Lieben Boot Factory," Merrick replied dutifully. "Foreclosed on five years ago, property still belongs to Archersville First National Bank. There have been several reports of unauthorized persons on the grounds, including one with a rotten face."

"A ghoul?" Chase grimaced.

Ghouls were people on the brink of death who had their souls bound to a copy of their old body before passing. They fell under the branch of necromancy legislature and were a felony with severe consequences. Aiding in the creation of a ghoul or being raised as one meant decades in prison.

The practice was rare since the government had destroyed all trace of the necessary rites, but rogue witches like Sages were able to pass them down in secret through family grimoires. Ghouls could last for a while, but they were always eventually caught when their bodies began to rot.

"Possibly," Merrick said. "That's why we are going to check it out."

"Figured it had to be something fun."

"Fun? What do you mean by fun?"

"Magical, weird, and illegal," Chase explained. "Being magic enforcement means that whatever we're being sent out on is gonna be all three. It's not like we get cases for assault and battery. No, we get the magical assault where some crazy guy tried to whack some other guy's head off with a hammer made of ice."

"I do not recall that particular case."

"It's just an example. I meant I knew there was more going on than regular ol' trespassing."

"Why did you not say so, then?"

Chase sighed and shielded his eyes from the sun.

Yup. This frustrating man was the love of his life.

The rest of the drive was silent, and Chase's throbbing head was thankful for the quiet. When they pulled up to the old factory, he tried to focus through the pounding. He needed to be on high alert now.

If this really was a ghoul, they had to be careful. Decomposing or not, they were some nasty things to deal with—strong, fast, and usually very stinky.

Merrick slowly pulled the car around, making a full circle before coming back up front to park.

The factory was at least six stories tall, with a row of high windows on the bottom floor and corroded aluminum siding all over. There were several dumpsters full of big metal sheets, perhaps from when someone was trying to clear out the interior for scrap. The job had been abandoned, and what was left behind was a nasty-looking collection of thick, jagged metal.

There was a long row of windows on the top floor centered above the front door, and the dumpsters were positioned below, next to the door.

Chase suspected the factory's offices must have been located up there, and he tapped Merrick's arm when a shadow in one of the windows caught his eye.

"What is it?" Merrick asked.

"Saw someone," Chase said, still focused on the windows. "One person, maybe two. Whoever they are, we're not gonna be surprising them."

Merrick looked around the vacant parking lot again. "No cars. Not even a bicycle."

"Maybe they're a jumper."

"Do you mean a person who is suicidal or a person who possesses the ability to create portals?" Merrick made a face at the slang.

"The portal kind."

Creating portals was a rare form of magic, but not unheard of. It was highly regulated because of obvious safety hazards, not to mention its potential to be abused for criminal purposes. There were only two people in the city who were registered to jump. One was a baker in her seventies, the other was a professor....

Shit. What was his name? Chase felt like he knew it, but it left his mind as quickly as he could summon it.

"A ghoul with that particular ability is very unlikely," Merrick argued.

"Ghouls can still cast magic," Chase countered stubbornly. "You don't know."

"No, I do not. And that is what I do not like. We could be walking into anything."

"Yeah, well, maybe it's a bunch of kids screwing around." Chase shrugged, glancing over at Merrick to catch the familiar wrinkle of his brow that meant he was worried.

"Something does not feel right," Merrick said at last. "We should proceed with caution."

"Always do, Merry," Chase agreed. He didn't feel too great about walking into this place either, and being hungover certainly didn't help.

They exited the car together and headed to the front door.

Chase held out his index fingers and thumbs to form a triangle, murmuring the words for a perception spell to check the doorway before they went in. He was an ordinary fire discipline, and he still had to chant out the words to cast even the simplest spells. "Shit."

"What?"

"It's warded," Chase replied grumpily. "Very fancy protection spells out the ass. Definitely not some fuckin' kids. I haven't seen some of these glyphs before."

Merrick held up his hand for his own perception spell. He was able to look through the index finger and thumb of one hand without saying the words because having a flawless performance record, perfect physical exams, and more service commendations than anyone else on the force wasn't enough. He was gifted in the divine arts, the most powerful school of magic that both encompassed and surpassed all the others.

Merrick could cast with nothing but a flick of his wrist, while Chase had to mumble each syllable like a first grader learning to read.

Bastard really was perfect.

Perfect and apparently annoyed, as he was studying the wards with an unusual scowl.

"You recognize 'em?" Chase pressed.

"Yes. They are old. Very old." Merrick's scowl deepened. "They are wards of protection with Salgumel's blessing."

"God of Dreams, right?"

"Yes."

"So, that's bad?"

"Yes," Merrick sighed. "He was the ruler of the gods here on Aeon before they went into the dreaming."

"Right, right, went all crazy and ditched mankind for a big ol' nap."

Chase was a hopeful atheist—as in, hopefully he was wrong and he would manage to find some sort of faith before he croaked. His parents had been Lucian, but they were hardly devout. They never had Chase or his brother take the Litany, never had them baptized, nor did they ever participate in any Lucian communion.

Before they died, his parents had converted to the Sagittarian faith, the way of the Sages. The religion was a bit silly, based on fairy tales about monstrous gods with tentacles and swords made of starlight. His parents took their new beliefs very seriously, and Chase recalled they often spoke of the gods returning soon.

Whether it was the Lord of Light with his magical hands of pure sunshine or Great Azaethoth with his big horns and giant tentacles, Chase didn't put much stock in any of it. He'd tried to go to a Lucian service and even joined his parents in Sagittarian circles, and he always felt nothing.

Whatever was up there, Chase hadn't heard a peep.

"That is one interpretation," Merrick said with an oddly perturbed glare. "What is important here is that Salgumel's blessings are both powerful and corrupt."

"Restricted?" Chase frowned. Some forms of magic were illegal, like necromancy, but he wasn't sure about this Salgumel guy.

"I do not think there's been a modern occurrence of this particular spell to warrant any legislature."

"So what the fuck do we do?"

Merrick made a fist and squeezed. The frame of the door cracked, the wards broken in a snap. "We go through them."

As always, Chase was impressed and annoyed. He didn't understand how Merrick did half the things he saw him do. Damn divine magic.

Touched by starlight, as the Sages would say.

Lucian faith had shaped the modern magical system that was used to classify a person's abilities. They were either fire, water, earth, air, or divine.

The Sages had a far more complicated system to quantify magical skills. Chase's fire magic wasn't just fire; it was the fire of Shartorath's hearth, a bright and gentle flame that could heal and light a dark path.

It was good for lighting cigarettes and birthday candles, not so good for anything actually useful.

Like breaking protection sigils.

Wards removed, he and Merrick walked inside. The factory had been gutted, and all the machinery removed left it a vast and empty space. There was a single staircase leading up to the top floor, and Chase grimaced immediately.

"Flare?" Merrick asked in a hushed voice.

"You got it." Chase took the silencing flare from his belt, set it down by the bottom of the stairs, and activated it.

It would prevent spell casting of any kind in the immediate area, hopefully giving him and Merrick the upper hand against whatever was waiting for them upstairs. It also meant they couldn't cast, of course, but they had their guns. As advanced as magic was, primitive ballistics were still quite effective.

Up the stairs they went, Chase soon lagging behind. He was out of breath by the time they reached the top, cursing the eclair and every other baked good he'd ever eaten.

There was a single door in front of them, and Merrick cautiously reached for the knob. He paused to take out his gun, looking to Chase to confirm he was ready to charge in.

Chase could definitely hear movement and a few different voices now, and he removed his gun from its holster. He took a deep breath, nodding at Merrick as he whispered, "Go."

Merrick flung open the door, leading the charge inside as he shouted, "AVPD! You are all under arrest for trespassing on private property, a violation of general statute two point six—"

"Oh shit," Chase hissed, staring at the shit show they'd just walked into.

The office was big, dusty, and empty except for a few neglected desks, some large frames stacked up by the wall, and oh…

About eight men, all staring right at them.

None of them looked very friendly or happy to see them, and they were all definitely armed.

So much for a bunch of kids screwing around.

One of the men had a large bandage covering the side of his face, and he raised his hands as if to cast a spell. He scoffed in disgust when nothing happened.

"You have the right to remain silent," Merrick went on, totally fearless despite how outnumbered they were. "You have the right—"

"Kill them," Bandage Face ordered.

"Shit, shit, shit," Chase hissed, grabbing Merrick and pulling him down behind the closest desk as the men opened fire.

"Attacking law enforcement is a felony!" Merrick shouted, ducking down next to Chase with a snarl.

"Go! Go!" Bandage Face was shouting. "Take the paintings!"

Chase ducked his head down as bullets whizzed all around them, reaching for his phone. "We've gotta call for backup!"

"We cannot let them get away!" Merrick shouted as he leaned around the desk to fire back.

"What the fuck do you suggest we do, huh?" Chase demanded, gritting his teeth.

There was a loud explosion from somewhere outside the office, and then Chase heard the pop of a portal.

No, that was impossible.

"Stay here!" Merrick shouted, suddenly jumping up from the cover of the desk.

"Merrick! You dumb fuck! No!" Chase tried to grab him, but he wasn't fast enough. He saw a portal in the corner of the room, watching in shock as the gunmen began to retreat through it.

Bandage Face was still firing, and Merrick went right for him. He took him to the ground, and both of their weapons went flying. As they struggled, the bandage was ripped away, and Chase saw a rotten hole in the man's face.

Fuck, it was shaped like a hand.

Chase was up, firing into the portal at the retreating men to cover Merrick as he fought with Bandage Face. He didn't understand how a portal could have been opened while the silencing flare was up, but he didn't have time to question it.

Bandage Face managed to get an arm free from Merrick's grasp, hissing a chant and raising his hand for a spell. Light was bubbling up all around his fingers, but he wasn't directing it at Merrick.

It was aimed right at Chase.

"Chase, look out!" Merrick shouted, letting go of Bandage Face and turning to grab the glowing ball of energy.

It exploded, and the next thing Chase saw was the ceiling as he landed flat on his back. Merrick had flown backward from the blast, crashing into the window, glass shattering as he fell right through.

"Merrick!" Chase screamed, his ears ringing as he fought to get to his feet. He ran to the window, looking down at the ground below.

Oh fuck.

Merrick had hit the dumpster full of scrap metal, and he was…. No!

Chase forgot all about Bandage Face, racing back down the stairs as fast as he could. He barely noticed the pieces of the silencing flare as he sprinted by them, his heart in his throat as he burst through the front doors.

Merrick had to be okay.

He had to be!

Chase skidded to a stop when he found Merrick, dropping to his knees with an anguished sob.

Merrick's body was nearly split in half across his middle from where it had struck the giant sheets of metal, and there were loops of guts hanging out. His eyes were closed, and he wasn't moving.

Chase knew he needed to call someone. He had to call this in. But he felt too sick, his eyes filling with tears as he reached out to touch Merrick's face with trembling fingers.

He should have been faster, reacted quicker; he should have done something, anything....

Now he'd never have the chance to tell Merrick how he really felt.

Chase forced himself to look up at Merrick's torso again, sniffling miserably. It was then he noticed there wasn't any blood. There wasn't a single drop. What Chase had thought were guts and intestines were in fact....

Tentacles.

Thick, writhing green tentacles.

"What the fucking fuck," Chase whispered.

"Language," Merrick scolded as his eyes fluttered open. "Chase, get a hold of yourself."

"You.... You...." Chase jerked his hand away, nearly hysterical. "How... how are you even talking right now?"

"So," Merrick said, surprisingly calm for someone whose body was nearly in two pieces, "we may need to have a talk about what and who I really am."

"No fuckin' shit!"

Merrick looked annoyed, pulling his lower half down from where it was caught on the edge of the dumpster. His body began to mend back together, tentacles vanishing back inside, and he stood up and brushed himself off. "Profanity is unacceptable, Chase. I have told you—"

"Fuck that!" Chase shouted as he backed away in horror. "I'll use whatever fuckin' language I fuckin' want to! What the fuck are you?"

Merrick bowed his head, sighing heavily. He looked back up at Chase, and his eyes had turned into black pools scattered with thousands of little lights—no, with *stars*—and he said:

"I'm a god."

CHAPTER 2.

"A GOD?" Chase repeated.

Merrick seemed more concerned with the state of his shirt, sighing at the torn fabric. He shook his head as he brushed by Chase to go back inside the factory. "Yes, a god."

"What… I…." Chase wiped at his eyes as he struggled to make sense of this. "The tentacles, that's… those are real. You're a god. A Sagittarian god."

"Yes," Merrick said flatly, urging Chase to follow him inside. "Now come on. I may be able to track the portal's path, and we can follow them."

"Hold the fuck up!" Chase snapped, right on Merrick's heels as he led them back to the stairs. "Will you wait a fucking second? You don't get to fall out of fucking windows, make me think you're dead, and just act like, oops, it's not a big deal 'cause you're a god! Not without answering some questions!"

"Fine," Merrick said, turning around to face Chase in a huff. "I am Gordoth the Untouched, brother of Salgumel, Shartorath, Yeris, Ulgon, Elgrirath, Zarnorach, Xarbon, Solmach, Eb, Ebb, Ebbeth, and Lozathin. I was spawned by Baub, the child of Zunnerath and Halandrach, they who were born of Etheril and Xarapharos, descended directly from Great Azaethoth himself."

"Gordoth." Chase drew a blank. "And he's the god of what again?"

"Justice and righteous wrath!" Merrick replied shortly. He pointed down at the floor. "Look, the flare was destroyed. Our new friends must be using some sort of powerful artifact. It was how they were able to destroy the flare from such a great distance."

"Fuck, that's how they summoned the portal?" Chase finally took in the shattered pieces. "I've never heard of anything powerful enough to break a silencing flare like this before."

"I have, but it is old. Very old, like the protection wards they were using." Merrick headed up the stairs. "They must have found a rare cache of ancient magic somewhere."

"They? You mean ghoul face and company?"

"Yes, but he is not a ghoul. He is human. I do not know the source of his decomposition. It is a magic that I am not familiar with but—"

"Can we get back to the whole you being a god thing for a fuckin' second?"

"Later," Merrick said briskly.

"Hey!" Chase hated how out of breath he was, but he managed to catch Merrick's arm at the top of the stairs. "You asshole, I thought you were dead! Do you have any fuckin' idea how scared I was?"

Merrick flinched, but he didn't pull away. "I did not mean to worry you. As you can see, I am perfectly fine."

"Start talking," Chase demanded, giving Merrick's arm a firm tug. "Why the fuck is a god down here playing cops and robbers?"

Merrick made a face. "I suppose I owe you an explanation. I have been very dishonest about my identity."

"No shit." Chase let go and crossed his arms over his broad chest. "Was there ever even a real Benjamin Merrick?"

"Yes, there was." Merrick looked sad. "He was a brave man, a dedicated follower, and a seeker of justice."

"Was?" Chase felt sick.

"He prayed to me daily," Merrick explained. "He was a great champion of the law, and I woke up from the dreaming to help him often. I led him to victory many times, but it was my pride that killed him. He wanted to defeat the Luchesi cartel—"

"The Luchesi Massacre," Chase blurted out. Of all the stories told about Merrick's career, it was one of the most infamous. "You walked in on what was supposed to be a money drop, but it was an arms deal. Thirty men and you. I always fuckin' wondered how the hell you made it out!"

"I did not," Merrick sighed. "At least, that is to say Merrick did not."

"Fuck."

"It was my pride that sent him there. I found out where a high-ranking member of the Luchesi family was going to be, and I gave him a vision of the location. I wanted the victory of this man's arrest as much as he did, and I was blinded by the glory it would bring to my name.

"Merrick died before I could save him, and I took over his body to punish those responsible for his murder. I grievously misunderstood the nature of the meeting, and I had sent him straight to his death. I could not abide the idea that such a great man's life was lost because of my arrogance… so…."

"You've been chilling in the driver's seat, pretending to be Merrick?" Chase concluded.

"His legacy should not have ended there," Merrick said stubbornly. "I was responsible, and I intend to see this through."

"Until when exactly?"

"Until I am satisfied I have given Merrick the legacy he deserves." Merrick sighed again. "I am now trusting you will be discreet about this. If the world finds out that old gods are walking amongst mortals, there will be a terrible panic."

"But you guys are real," Chase argued. "I mean, fuck! All of this time, I had no idea what to fuckin' believe in, and here you are!"

"Yes, here I am."

"That's it?" Chase scoffed. "This, this is some life-changing shit!"

"That I expect you to keep to yourself," Merrick said firmly. "If Great Azaethoth wanted the gods to make ourselves known to mankind again, he would rise himself. Until then, we must keep this between us."

Chase stared as Merrick walked back into the office, and he scrambled for something to say.

He could have made a joke about how at least he didn't need to feel bad about his paperwork since he was apparently being proofread by an immortal. He also seriously needed to look into the Sagittarian faith, because it was pretty sad he'd actually met a living god and had no idea who he was.

However, the only lingering thought he could focus on was how even more painfully out of his league Merrick was now.

It was bad enough when Merrick was a flesh-and-blood human, but now that he was a god?

No way.

"Are you coming?" Merrick called out.

"Yeah, yeah." Chase buried his heartache and hurried into the office, finding Merrick looking over the corner where the portal had been. "Anything?"

"No." Merrick scowled. "I cannot track the portal." He narrowed his eyes at Chase. "Perhaps if you had not been so distracted by my identity, I could have tried this while there was still some trace of it left."

"Wow." Chase smacked his lips. "That sort of sounds like you're blaming me."

"Because I am."

"Were you always this much of a prick?" Chase snapped. "Or is it because now I know who you are, you've let your hair down a bit? Decided to just go full asshole deity, huh?"

"Your judgment is clouded."

"Uh, yeah, a bit, because I'm still trying to get over seeing my partner split in fuckin' half!" Chase hated how easily his voice rose. "Tiny bit traumatizing!"

"I can only conclude the man I fought fled through the portal before it closed," Merrick went on, ignoring Chase. "There are still some frames over there, though I thought there were more when we first entered the room."

The stack of frames had been knocked over, and only three remained.

Chase kneeled down to lift one up, finding what was left of a painting. It looked and smelled like it had been dipped in paint thinner, and the original subject was indecipherable. The paint had been eaten away to reveal several long paragraphs of writing hidden beneath.

It wasn't in any language Chase had ever seen, and he checked the other paintings to find they were the same. "Any idea what this shit says, your godliness?"

"It is definitely godstongue," Merrick replied, kneeling down to take a closer look.

"Language written by the gods for the gods, right?"

"Yes."

"So, can you read it?"

"No."

"Why the hell not?" Chase stood up, letting the paintings fall back on the floor.

"It was not written for me," Merrick said, "but it must have been very important. Those men were willing to murder two officers to secure them."

"But not these," Chase pointed out.

"Perhaps they already had all the information they needed from these ones." Merrick's brow crinkled.

"What is it?"

"Hmm?"

"You've got your thinking face on."

"The old protection wards, the ability to destroy the silencing flare, and now these paintings that were obscuring godstongue that has not been read in hundreds of years," Merrick listed off carefully. "I believe these men are devoted to the worship of my brother Salgumel."

"Dream guy," Chase recalled.

"Yes." Merrick scowled. "I believe these may be part of a set of paintings commissioned by Lord Harrison Collins in the seventeenth century. There were eight in all, one for each of the Sagittarian holidays. One was stolen from auction last year, and I believe there were others taken from a warehouse."

"Yeah, hey, I remember that!" Chase exclaimed. "The auction got robbed after that fire took out the day center for the deaf and blind kids and the damn dog park."

"Forensics will be able to confirm if these are in fact those missing paintings." Merrick reached for his phone, patting his pocket. "I seem to have lost my phone."

"Down in the dumpster?"

"I am going to try and retrieve it," Merrick said. "We need to call this in. We need to confirm if these are Lord Collins's paintings as soon as possible."

"What's his deal?"

"He was reported to have hidden a ritual in the paintings that could awaken Salgumel." Merrick walked over to the broken window. "And before you ask, yes, it is bad. Most of my family sleeps very peacefully in the dreaming, but my brother has gone mad."

"Mad?" Chase's stomach turned. "Like crazy?"

"I believe he would destroy the world if he woke up and saw it in its current state," Merrick said, holding out his arm. From his coat sleeve, thick green tentacles spiraled downward, reaching to the dumpster below.

Trying not to stare, Chase stammered, "O-okay, so, so since those guys are big worshippers, I am gonna guess that they're cool with all of that."

"I do not want to make assumptions, but yes, I would say they are very 'cool' with it." Merrick's tentacles came back in, curled around what was left of his phone. The screen was shattered, and he gritted his teeth. "Ah, just great."

"I'll call." Chase got his phone, preparing to dial.

"And what are you going to tell them?"

"I'm not gonna say anything about you and your little tentacle swan dive, if that's what you're worried about. What, you don't trust me?"

"I do trust you," Merrick insisted. "I trust you with my life."

"That's rich considering you're immortal."

"But you did not know that, and you still went to great lengths to protect me." Merrick stood up straighter. "Your efforts have not gone without notice."

"My efforts," Chase echoed, not sure what to make of that. He caught himself staring at Merrick and grimaced, turning away to make the call.

"It is very much appreciated." Merrick boldly placed his hand on Chase's shoulder. "Please do not mistake my current frustration for any ill will toward you."

Chase put his hand over Merrick's, and his pulse pattered a little faster. "It's no big deal. Just, uh, you know, still trying to make sense of all this."

"I do not want our professional relationship to be affected," Merrick said, surprisingly earnest. "I am still Detective Benjamin Merrick."

"But also Gordock."

"Gordoth," Merrick corrected. "Please. I do not want your feelings about working with me to change."

Your feelings....

Swallowing around the lump in his throat, Chase forced a smile. "Don't worry. I don't think they could if you tried." He held up his phone. "Gimme a second?"

"Of course," Merrick said, stepping away to give him some space.

Chase informed dispatch of the situation and assured them no one was hurt. He left out any details about Merrick's true identity, and he did his best to give a description of Bandage Face and some of the other men.

After hanging up, Chase said, "All right, they're on their way."

"Thank you." Merrick offered a small smile.

"For what?"

"For showing me my trust in you was not misplaced." Merrick's smile broadened. "In spite of your questionable hygiene, your lack of punctuality, your intense hatred of spelling—"

"Yeah, yeah," Chase grumbled.

"—and I know you have not eaten anything that is not full of processed sugar in years—"

"Okay, okay!" Chase raised his voice. "I get it!"

"—but you are a wonderful human being," Merrick finished, stubbornly lifting his head. "It has been an honor dispatching justice to the wicked with you. You would make a splendid disciple."

"Thanks." Chase tried to take the compliment, but he only felt worse.

"What is wrong?" Merrick almost seemed to be pouting. "I did not mean to offend you."

"It's fine." Chase smirked. "Pretty high praise from a god, right?"

Merrick's grimace deepened.

"So," Chase said, tiptoeing to the broken window and glancing outside, "is it true you guys had tentacle orgies? Was that really a thing?"

"You have discovered I am an ancient immortal, and that is the first thing you ask me?" Merrick actually laughed.

"Well, yeah." Chase grinned. "Priorities."

"There were many fertility celebrations," Merrick replied. He sounded bashful. "It was common for worshippers to offer their bodies to us. Due to the nature of our anatomy, ahem, we can copulate with more than one mortal at a time."

"So, orgies."

"Of a religious nature."

"By anatomy, do you mean what I think you mean?" Chase had quite the imagination, but he was dying to hear details.

"Most of the gods have multiple appendages for mating." Merrick ducked his head. "Though we do not actually need a partner for reproduction."

"Where's the fun in that?" Chase teased.

Merrick laughed, smiling again. "My father, Baub, personally spawned thirteen of us in all."

"So you've got twelve siblings?"

"More still if you count my half brothers and sisters." Merrick cocked his head. "You really do not know anything about the gods, do you."

"No, not really," Chase admitted. "I know some of the names, I know a few holidays, and uh, that's about it. Definitely wanna hear more about the copulating."

"Now you are being obscene."

"What?" Chase grinned slyly. "I'm a heathen. I don't know any better. Educate me."

"No." Merrick's tone was firm, but he was smiling.

"Got it, you're not an easy god. I respect that." Chase winked. "Need to buy you dinner before you show me the tentacled goods."

"Detective Chase!" Merrick's eyes widened. "Are you... are you flirting with me?"

"Damn, you *are* a good detective."

"That is not acceptable behavior," Merrick scolded. "Is this because now you know I am a god, you expect me to be promiscuous?"

"What?" Chase huffed. "Come on."

"I told you that I did not want this to affect our working relationship," Merrick grumbled. "I expected better from you."

"I'm joking, for fuck's sake."

"Well, it is not funny," Merrick continued to complain. "The nature of my intimate parts is not up for discussion."

"For the record, I wanted to know all about your intimate parts *before* I found out you were a god," Chase said honestly.

Merrick didn't immediately respond, and he looked confused. "Are you referring to the clothing-optional invitation?"

"The one we've never, ever talked about?" Chase leaned against one of the desks. He didn't see any point in hiding his feelings now. "Yeah, that one."

"I am not here to partake in physical pleasures, no matter how tempting you may be."

"Wait, tempting?" Chase couldn't have heard him correctly. "You think I'm tempting?"

"Obviously," Merrick huffed. "It is why I had to refuse your advances that night. I cannot allow myself to become distracted by your sensual sorcery."

"Sensual what now?" Chase questioned if he was awake right now and almost pinched himself to check.

"It does not matter," Merrick hissed impatiently. "You are my partner, and it would be detrimental to Merrick's future in law enforcement to become sexually involved with a coworker."

"Okay, the speaking in third person is weird—"

"Do not bring this up again," Merrick snapped. "For my sake and Merrick's, I must insist you stop right now. I cannot risk damaging his legacy over physical pleasures. I do not know how else I can refuse you and make you understand."

"Listen to me," Chase pleaded, a flicker of hope rekindling inside of him and spurring him on. "I never thought in a million years that you'd ever be into me! I didn't have a clue! I don't just want physical pleasures, okay? I'm sure that's all super great with your tentacles and appendages or whatever, but I'm—"

"Detective Chase, please," Merrick said firmly, holding up his hands for silence. He shook his head, his face contorting in pain. "Please stop."

The words were right on the tip of Chase's tongue.

But I'm in love with you, you big, beautiful idiot!

He couldn't bring himself to say it, seeing how upset Merrick already was, and he fell silent. His mind was still reeling from learning that Merrick had found him attractive all of this time—What the hell was sensual sorcery anyway?—and he planned to ride that stroke to his ego and hold on to it for as long as he could.

It wasn't a confession of undying affection, but it was much more than he ever thought he would have.

Chase heard some car doors shut, and he looked outside through the broken window. He did his best to remain calm in spite of his turbulent emotions, announcing, "Our guys are here."

"Good," Merrick said, taking a deep breath as if to collect himself. "We must make haste. Those men have a ritual that may bring about the end of the world."

"I'll go get 'em." Chase headed downstairs before Merrick could argue. He needed to get some distance and clear his head. Finding out the guy he was in love with was actually a god was taking some time to process.

Not to mention that said god found him so very tempting but wasn't interested in a relationship.

How disgustingly ironic.

"Hey there!" Milo Evans, one of their forensic techs, greeted him at the front door. He was round and bearded, not too much unlike Chase, although much younger. "How's it going?"

"Fine," Chase said more abruptly than he meant to as he brushed by. "Follow the stairs. Merrick is up there."

"Okay, grumpy," Milo said with a pout.

"Aww, is somebody having a bad day?" Daisy Lopez asked sweetly, right on Milo's heels. She was another forensic technician with a chipper attitude to match her festive pigtails.

She was also a rampant pastry hog if Merrick was to be believed.

"You should be celebrating! You might have just recovered Lord Collins's paintings!" Daisy went on with a bright smile. "Do you have any idea how freakin' cool that is? More than enough of a reason to turn that mean ol' frown upside down!"

"Well, he did get shot at," Milo warned. "Maybe leave Big Red alone for right now?"

"Do you need a hug, Detective Chase?" Daisy frowned. "You don't look so great."

"I'm just ducky," Chase muttered, continuing on to Merrick's car. He found the pack of cigarettes stashed in the glove box and lit one up with a small flame produced by a snap of his fingers.

Ignis vitae, the one and only spell he could cast without speaking.

Merrick didn't smoke, but he knew Chase did and liked to have one on particularly stressful days.

Thoughtful jerk god.

Chase was on his third when Merrick came down to find him.

"Milo and Daisy are going to be processing the scene for the rest of the afternoon," Merrick said. "They have already recovered several sets of prints, and they hope to identify some of our suspects soon. APB has already been issued based on our descriptions."

"Those guys could already be out of the city by now." Chase sighed.

"Portal ranges for humans are very limited. Even the most talented mortal witches can only travel a few hundred yards."

"Yeah, I know, we puny humans have these stupid limitations—" Chase rolled his eyes. "—but all they gotta do is jump over to the nearest car and boom, they got wheels."

"I do not think they will leave the city," Merrick said carefully.

"Why not?"

"There is a weakness here."

"What kinda weakness?"

"In the veil that separates Aeon from the worlds beyond," Merrick replied, dropping his voice. "About two decades ago, it was fractured. If someone wanted to reach the other side into Zebulon, where the gods are sleeping, this would be an optimal location."

"Oh, goody." Chase took a long drag of his cigarette. "So, let's say they're staying here. We still have no idea where to find them. And don't you dare bring up your bullshit 'I coulda traced the portal' crap."

Merrick audibly clicked his teeth together, as if to stop himself from saying just that. He cleared his throat. "Well, what do you propose, then? We are at a loss until Mr. Evans and Miss Lopez are able to divulge any findings from the evidence."

"What about the paintings?" Chase asked. "Maybe there's a clue in this ritual, like a location or something. Maybe it has to be done by a river or in a circle of oak trees. Something specific that could help us figure out where they might be."

"I believe it is the godstongue of Salgumel," Merrick said sullenly. "I do not know anyone, god or mortal, who would be able to translate it. The department's linguist quit, remember?"

"Yeah, I know." Chase's stomach turned. "Real shame. He was a good kid."

"I doubt that he would have been able to translate the godstongue, but it would have been nice to have the option. I wonder if we can look him up—"

"Hey, there was this professor who had a huge boner for Salgumel...." Chase felt a stabbing pain in his head and clutched his temples. "Fuck!"

"What is the matter?" Merrick made as if to reach for Chase but pulled away.

"There's something wrong with me." Chase gasped as his entire head started pounding. He dropped his cigarette, and he had to lean against the car to steady himself.

The harder he tried to remember, the worse the pain got until he was nearly in tears.

"May I touch you, Detective Chase?" Merrick asked urgently. "I wish to help you."

"Yeah, fine! Fuck! Whatever!"

Merrick stepped right into Chase's space and put his hand on his chest.

Chase gasped when the smooth flesh of one of Merrick's tentacles slipped in between the buttons of his shirt to meet bare skin. He felt an incredible joy he'd never experienced before, a bliss that brought on a fresh wave of tears and made his knees weak. He grabbed onto Merrick's shoulders to brace himself, and he almost sobbed.

"Breathe, Detective Chase," Merrick soothed. "It is almost over."

The pain faded away, and Chase found he could think more clearly. This wasn't just Merrick touching him—no, this was a god, an immortal being of unimaginable strength, and Chase could sense the echoes of an ancient power that made him feel like a tiny little ant in comparison.

Merrick's eyes had become black again, two endless voids full of millions of stars. It was overwhelming to touch something so divine, and the tender way Merrick was gazing at him made the moment even sweeter. If Chase had any lingering doubts about what Merrick truly was, they would have been all gone now.

Chase managed to break out of the euphoric daze before he got too emotional, but not before teasing, "You know, you can call me Elwood when your hand is down my shirt."

"My apologies… I…," Merrick sputtered. "I was just… I wanted to help!"

"Don't worry about it," Chase said, enjoying Merrick's embarrassment.

"Has your pain receded?"

"Yeah, thanks."

"Someone tried to erase your memory," Merrick said as he backed away. "I believe I have removed what was blocking you."

"Salgumel. Right. Yeah! There was this professor named Emil Kunst who was a fuckin' expert on him, and…." Chase took a deep breath as it all came rushing back to him. "That son of a bitch! And he took my fuckin' badge!"

"What?" Merrick was startled.

"You got a nephew named Azaethoth?"

"Azaethoth the Lesser." Merrick blinked. "Why?"

"Because I'm about to go kick his godly ass!"

CHAPTER 3.

"So," Merrick said as he speedily drove them back into the city, "my nephew is inside the ghoul of a thief named Lochlain Fields. He is in the company of disgraced former detective Sloane Beaumont, and they may have killed the professor?"

"I knew something weird was going on!" Chase growled. "Remember when we kept running into them? Like seeing Sloane over at the funeral home where the ghoul body went missing?"

"And at the precinct when Mr. Evans was escorting Mr. Beaumont and those other strangers around despite my objections?"

"Yeah, the ginger pretty boy was Lochlain Fields. Or actually Azaethoth. Can't you tell if somebody is a god or not?"

"Not if they are hiding their aura. We can blend in as mortals very well." Merrick scoffed to himself. "It makes me wonder who the 'love goddess' was now. Perhaps another wayward relative of mine."

"The love of your life is right in front of you. You just have to be brave enough to take it."

Chase remembered the prediction verbatim now, but she couldn't have meant....

"What led you to confronting Mr. Beaumont?" Merrick asked, interrupting Chase's thoughts.

"Okay, so I figured out the missing ghoul from the funeral home was Lochlain Fields after I ran the prints, and that was mighty odd since he's not actually dead," Chase replied quickly. "He and his new hubby got some property that belonged to Professor Kunst, property Sloane inherited from him after his very mysterious death."

"Mysterious?"

"Went missing for months until he was declared dead, and the death certificate said some bullshit about him dying at home."

"Ah."

"Oh, but there's more." Chase held up a finger. "Yours truly went into the file and found a redacted report that his rotten corpse was actually found out in the woods on his property. Isn't that fun? Then, of all fuckin' things, his body was cremated with no medical examiner authorization!"

"And Professor Kunst was a Sage, yes?" Merrick made a face. "He should have been shrouded and buried."

"Well, he was technically buried once. Just, you know, in a grave of the shallow variety."

"And Mr. Beaumont was involved in his demise?"

"Pretty fuckin' sure. That's why I went to go talk to him to get some damn answers. That's when that bastard Azaethoth erased my memory!"

"And you made no mention of this to me?" Merrick frowned. "Not a word prior to going to see him?"

Swallowing down a lump in his throat, Chase replied, "No, I didn't."

"And why not?"

"Milo and Sloane are real good friends, and we all used to work together, you know? I never thought what the department did to him was right, and I figured I could at least give him a chance to explain himself."

"Even though you suspect him of murder?"

"Only a little!" Chase argued. "I really don't think Sloane did it, but I knew he was mixed up in it. It was probably your boy Azaethoth! He's the one who messed up my brain! And that asshole took my badge!"

"My nephew is many things, but I find it difficult to believe he would murder a mortal. He is a thief, yes, but not a killer. He is not that kind of a god."

"Well, Sloane ain't that kinda guy."

"He had the perfect motive," Merrick protested. "Or did you forget that Professor Kunst was the one who murdered his parents?"

"No, I didn't forget," Chase snapped. "That case is why Sloane got fired! He'd been working on it for years—"

"But he suddenly receives a taped confession to close the case right *before* Professor Kunst happens to go missing? And after he is declared dead, he just happens to leave everything to Mr. Beaumont?"

"I'm sure there's an explanation," Chase said stubbornly.

"It is motive."

"Yeah, well, we'll see."

"Motive you withheld," Merrick accused. "Your dishonesty is extremely unethical, and it undermines the trust between us—"

"Oh, that's real cute, coming from the guy who was lying all this time about being a god!" Chase snapped more harshly than he meant to. "How's that for undermining trust, huh?"

Merrick was clearly stung, saying nothing as he refocused his attention on the road.

The rest of the drive was silent, and Chase had the weirdest sensation of déjà vu when they pulled into Sloane's humble apartment complex. He wasn't looking forward to this, but he trusted his gut.

Sloane wasn't a killer.

After Merrick parked the car, Chase led the way to Sloane's building and knocked on his front door.

Chase's heart was pounding while they waited for him to answer, and he wiped his forehead with his sleeve. He was nervous about possibly facing off against the god who wiped his memory, but then he felt a small nudge from Merrick.

"I am here," Merrick said, perhaps hoping to alleviate Chase's obvious stress.

"I know," Chase said in reply. Though the concern was touching and having another god at his side was reassuring, he still wasn't sure how to feel about all of this.

He'd woken up this morning like any other, hungover and alone. In only a few hours, he'd found out the Sages' gods were real, his memory had been tampered with, and a bunch of crazy witches were actively trying to wake up one of those old gods to destroy the world.

Not to mention the man he actively worshipped wasn't a man at all, but a member of the same ancient immortal family.

The door opened, and Sloane Beaumont was on the other side. He was a handsome young man with black hair and thick eyebrows. Both of those bushy monsters were raised in definite surprise when he saw Chase and Merrick standing on his doorstep.

"Oh!" Sloane blinked. "Hey, Chase. Detective Merrick. Uh, what can I do for you?"

"Who is it?" a voice called from inside the apartment. "Is it the mailman? Because we have unfinished business!"

"I remember everything," Chase said sternly, enjoying the sudden look of terror on Sloane's face, "and now we are all gonna sit down and have a nice little chat together. And hey, I want my badge back too."

"Uh, Loch?" Sloane called out urgently, backpedaling inside. "We have company."

Chase stepped in first, and Merrick shut the door behind them.

Loch or Azaethoth or whoever he was got up from the couch where he'd been lounging and joined Sloane. He was an attractive redhead with a twinkle of mischief in his eye, laughing when he saw them.

"It's you two again." He eyeballed Merrick. "Were you ever able to have anything done about the stick up your—"

"Yeah, it's us," Chase cut in. "Now, are you the god or the thief?"

"Mmm, both?" Loch shrugged. "Being the god of thieves certainly qualifies me."

"Loch!" Sloane hissed. "Think first! Then talk!"

"Look, whatever little mind-zapping you did is gone," Chase declared, staring Sloane down. "I wanna know what the hell really happened to Professor Emil Kunst and why that guy there is prancing around in a ghoul of a man who ain't dead."

"Okay, okay," Sloane said, holding up his hands. "You guys just wanna talk, we can talk, but I don't think you're gonna believe me—"

"Well, what's stopping me from zapping their memories, hmm?" Loch challenged, narrowing his eyes and grinning like a cat about to pounce. "That seemed to work well before."

"Because I will stop you," Merrick said as he stepped forward to face Loch, "and you never could beat me at anything... Azzath."

Loch was immediately confused, and he stared at Merrick for a long moment. "Uncle Gordoth? Is that... is that really you?"

"I am Gordoth," Merrick recited, "brother of Salgumel, Shartorath, Yeris, Ulgon, Elgrirath, Zarnorach, Xarbon, Solmach, Eb, Ebb, Ebbeth, and Lozathin. I was spawned by Baub, the child of Zunnerath and

Halandrach, they who were born of Etheril and Xarapharos, descended directly from Great Azaethoth himself."

"Uncle Gordoth! This is where you've been? Hiding out in a mortal vessel?" Loch laughed and grabbed Merrick in a big hug. Both of their tentacles wrapped around each other, their voices overlapping excitedly.

"Look how much you've grown—"

"I've missed you! We tried to find you for the wedding!"

"I missed you as well. It has been too long! Wait, wedding?"

"Too long, far too long! And yes! My wedding!"

"God of justice," Sloane murmured. He seemed pretty calm for someone watching two gods hugging it out.

"Yup. God of justice. That's him." Chase leaned in to catch Sloane's ear. "And Azaethoth is...?"

"God of thieves and divine retribution." Sloane smiled hesitantly. "Uh, I'm guessing you didn't know about Merrick...?"

"No." Chase watched how openly Merrick smiled with Loch, and he brushed off a quick pinch of jealousy.

As the immortals finally parted, Merrick smacked the back of Loch's head with one of his tentacles.

"Ow!" Loch pouted. "What was that for?"

"Erasing a mortal's memory," Merrick scolded.

"Owwww!" Loch cried, trying to duck the next bop.

"It was unjustified, immature, and sloppy!" Merrick continued to rant. "What if Detective Chase's memories returned on their own and he came back to arrest you?"

"Zap, zap memories again?" Loch suggested. "I certainly wasn't going to let him take me or my mate to prison! Pffft!"

Merrick raised a tentacle as if to hit him again.

"Can we get to the part where you guys explain what the hell is going on?" Chase grumbled.

"I did it to protect Sloane," Loch said stubbornly. "He is my mate, and we have a family to think of now!"

Sloane's face became a startlingly bright shade of red.

"You have truly taken this man as your mate?" Merrick sounded skeptical.

"Mother really tried to find you to wake you for the wedding!" Loch fussed. "I wanted you to be there."

"I am sorry I missed it," Merrick said sincerely.

"You should be. It was spectacular. Very big fire." Loch beamed. "Mmm, no orgy, but still very nice. Sloane is now my mate. We've just celebrated our two-month anniversary."

"Congratulations, that's great," Chase huffed as he stalked over to the living room. He plopped down on the edge of the coffee table, gesturing to the couch. "Now. I'd like to have my badge back and get some answers, if you'd be so kind."

"Loch?" Sloane prompted.

"Must I?" Loch asked.

"Yes."

Loch pouted, but he produced the badge, dangling it from one of his tentacles for Chase.

"Thank you," Chase said shortly as he shoved it in his jacket pocket. "Now, let's talk, huh?"

"Right," Sloane said, taking a deep breath and grabbing a seat on the couch across from Chase. "It all started last Dhankes when I went to Milo's Halloween party."

"*Milo* Milo? Our Milo? He knows about this shit?"

"Yeah, look. It all started at his party. That's where I met Lochlain Fields. We chatted for a minute, I gave him my card—"

"They wanted to mate," Loch explained in a dramatic whisper as he sat down next to Sloane.

"No! We were planning to go on a date."

"I understand these things to be the same."

"They are not. Anyway. Later that night, Lochlain was murdered. He'd stolen a piece of a totem for Professor Emil Kunst, a totem that could wake up Salgumel. Tollmathan came after Lochlain, and—"

"Tollmathan, my nephew?" Merrick frowned, looking to Loch worriedly for confirmation.

Loch nodded.

"Yes," Sloane replied grimly. "Kunst performed a ritual with my parents nineteen years ago that was supposed to destroy this totem.

Something went horribly wrong. It broke the totem into fragments and then scattered them all over Aeon instead of turning them to dust.

"Kunst survived the ritual and spent the rest of his life trying to find those broken pieces. He wanted to restore the totem to destroy it once and for all. He found out Toll was trying to get it, too, and figured he could stop him if he had at least one piece."

"The piece Lochlain Fields stole for him?" Chase asked.

"Right. Toll went after Lochlain to get it, and well, it didn't end well for him. That's when—"

"That's when I woke up," Loch chimed in proudly. "Lochlain is a very devoted follower of mine, an absolutely brilliant thief. I heard his prayers that night, and I came to visit him. Unfortunately, he had already been murdered by the time I arrived. I took over his dead body—"

"Why is that a thing with you guys?" Chase mumbled, side-eyeing Merrick.

"—and I found Sloane's card in his pocket. He agreed to help me find Lochlain's murderer and offered to mate with me and carry my hot seed—"

Blushing, Sloane quickly spoke over him, "We figured out it was Tollmathan who was behind everything, and he ended up with all the totem pieces. Loch and Kunst managed to steal it back, and we conducted the same ritual to destroy it." He glanced at his feet. "But there's a cost, you see, a blood sacrifice to power the necessary magic."

"Lemme guess," Chase piped up. "Kunst paid up?"

"He wanted to make amends for how my parents died," Sloane said, smiling sadly. "It was the failed ritual that killed them, and he felt responsible. He offered his life to power the spell. His sacrifice stopped Tollmathan from using the totem, and it... well...." He stopped to clear his throat.

Loch wrapped a few tentacles around Sloane's waist and pulled him in close. "Once the totem was destroyed, my beloved mate and I battled Toll to the death."

"My sincerest condolences." Merrick frowned, offering his tentacles to Loch. "Taking your brother's life could not have been easy for you."

"Oh, I didn't do it," Loch said. "It was Sloane." He held his head high, positively glowing with pride. "My mate is a Starkiller."

Merrick immediately pulled back his tentacles and stared at Sloane as if he might bite. "Truly?"

"He is the very first since Abigail," Loch bragged. "Great Azaethoth blessed him with a sword of starlight to vanquish Tollmathan, doubtlessly because our love is legendary and is destined to be written in the stars above for all time."

Chase couldn't quite place the odd expression on Merrick's face—anger, shock, or perhaps even fear? He hated being so ignorant, but he had to ask, "And a Starkiller is what now?"

"A mortal with the power to kill a god," Merrick replied.

"Well, fuck." Chase leaned back. "I'm gonna guess that doesn't happen too often, right? Like lightning never strikes the same place twice kinda thing?"

"Oh, but it did happen twice," Loch said.

"Who?" Merrick demanded.

"Gronoch," Sloane replied, surprisingly miserable in spite of being an apparently all-powerful god-killing witch. "He also tried to wake up Salgumel and build an army for him. Well, he tried to make one anyway."

"Gronoch?" Chase asked, thinking about making flash cards later.

"God of healing and attrition," Merrick dutifully explained. "Second oldest of Salgumel's sons, my nephew, Azzath's brother."

"Got it."

"What kind of army was he trying to create?" Merrick asked, hovering beside the couch.

"Gronoch had followers in Xenon steal enough Asran bones to force a god's soul to astral project and leave their immortal body," Sloane said. "He then attached the god's soul to a mortal. Essentially, the mortal was then able to puppeteer all the god's powers and control them."

Chase didn't understand most of what Sloane had said, but he was quick to point out, "But you can't bind two living souls together like that. It would be way too much magic for one body!"

"You can if the mortal is Silenced," Sloane explained. "And, well, use a couple hundred binding spells."

"Did he succeed?" Merrick asked.

"Only once we know of."

"A very angry little mortal named Alexander," Loch said with a roll of his eyes. "Smokes way too much, such a terrible habit."

"And the god bound to him?" Merrick pressed.

"Called himself Rota," Loch replied. "He couldn't remember who he was, and I didn't recognize him."

"He was definitely old," Sloane said. "He and Alexander together were very powerful."

Loch scoffed and mumbled under his breath, "Not *that* powerful."

Sloane patted Loch's thigh, looking to Chase and Merrick as he explained, "Gronoch was using Alexander and Rota to kidnap more potential subjects for the army. They were using the Hazel Research Group as a base of operations for the experiments."

"The big medical place that went belly up a few months ago?" Chase remembered seeing it on the news and heard the rumors flying all over the precinct. "There was a big fire at their building downtown. Feds were all over it. No local cops were allowed in."

"That was you two, wasn't it?" Merrick accused.

"Yes," Loch said shamelessly. "Oh, and Alexander and Rota, of course. And sweet Galgareth, my dear sister."

"She was there?" Merrick was alarmed. "How did you even get involved in all of this?"

"They were going after a client of mine," Sloane replied. "Jay Tintenfisch."

"Jay?" Chase's eyes widened. "Little IT guy Jay from the AVPD? Is that why he went on fuckin' leave for so long?"

"Yes," Sloane confirmed. "We were trying to protect him from Alexander and Rota. Once they found out I was a Starkiller, they wanted me to help them fight Gronoch instead."

"Ah, to serve justice for his crimes," Merrick said with a nod. "A worthy quest."

"Not quite that noble." Sloane smiled sadly. "They wanted Gronoch to tell them where Rota's body was."

"Didn't it die after his soul got yanked out?" Chase asked. "I mean, you know, eventually?"

"No. He's a god. His body won't die no matter how long his soul is separated from it, and breaking the binding circles to free him could kill Alexander."

"But then Rota would be able to reclaim his body," Merrick said, wrinkling his brow.

"Yes, but not in enough time to save Alexander," Sloane explained. "They're, well, they're sort of a thing. A romantic thing."

"That can't mate," Loch whispered loudly. "I believe that's why Alexander is so angry."

"Ah, I see. Rota will not break the bindings without his body being close enough to ensure that he can heal Alexander." Merrick nodded in understanding. "Well, if you killed Gronoch, were they successful?"

"We don't know," Sloane said, glancing at Loch. "We haven't seen or heard from them since Gronoch died. He told them Rota's body was at the Fountain of the Kindress, and they took—"

"Sloane made out with them," Loch chimed in.

"Loch!" Sloane was mortified. "You don't have to tell everyone that!"

"Wait, wait!" Merrick pinched the bridge of his nose, a sign of frustration Chase knew well. "The Kindress? Really?"

Chase held up his hand like they were in class. "And that is who now?"

"Great Azaethoth's legendary firstborn son," Merrick replied, still pinching hard. "A being of absolute destruction that is reborn only to die again through an endless cycle perpetuated by Great Azaethoth's grief."

"Uh-huh." Chase wasn't just going to need flash cards, he was going to need a damn tutor. "So, basically, all of Salgumel's kids are taking turns trying to destroy everything by waking his old ass up?"

"Yes." Sloane fidgeted, reaching for Loch's tentacles and squeezing. "With an unknown number of other gods supporting his return too."

"We have reason to believe there has been a resurgence in Salgumel's mortal followers as well," Merrick said with a frown.

"How so?"

"Freaky-ass paintings were discovered written in godstongue that are rumored to contain a ritual to wake ol' Sally boy up," Chase explained. "Fun stuff."

"Do you guys need help?" Sloane perked up.

"We'll be happy to give you an excellent discount, on account of being family and all," Loch said, grunting when Sloane elbowed him.

"No," Merrick said sternly. "Your previous efforts to preserve this world are appreciated, although I have nearly lost count of how many laws you have violated—"

"Crazy-ass people and old gods are trying to fuck all of humanity with no lube, and you're worried about that?" Chase scolded.

"I am still an officer of the law," Merrick said indignantly.

"What are you guys going to do, then?" Sloane asked.

"Guess try to find somebody who can read this godstongue nonsense," Chase replied, scratching his beard.

"No! About all of the law breaking!" Sloane scowled. "Kinda wanna know if I need to be worried about being arrested."

"My uncle is not going to arrest you," Loch insisted. "And even if he does, I'll visit you in prison every day."

"Not funny."

"We will not make any arrests," Merrick replied, making little effort to not sound disappointed. "Protecting this world supersedes my mortal duties as a police officer, and having a Starkiller incarcerated would deny us a great ally."

"Plus, I would be very mad at you," Loch huffed.

"That as well." Merrick rolled his eyes. "But do not think this gives you two permission to do as you please. From now on, I will expect you to inform me of any pertinent news regarding my brother and anyone or anything trying to hasten his return."

"Absolutely," Sloane agreed, though he quickly added, "as long as you agree to share info with us too. We're all in this together now."

"I will think about it." Merrick's upper lip twitched.

"Well, then we'll think about keeping you informed," Loch countered sweetly.

"Azzath," Merrick warned.

"Gordoth," Loch sniped, mimicking Merrick's grumpy tone. "Mother was right. You really do have a stick inside of you."

Chase snorted and covered his mouth to stifle a laugh.

Merrick glared at him.

"That love goddess, she was your mother?" Chase cleared his throat. "She was a fuckin' hoot."

"Urilith," Merrick confirmed. "Azzath's mother and my sister-in-law." He looked to Sloane. "As long as you do not compromise any active investigation or risk potential exposure, we will help you. An equal exchange of information."

"Wonderful!" Loch exclaimed.

"Who else is aware of our presence here on Aeon? Mr. Evans, Mr. Tintenfisch, yes, but who else?"

"The Super Secret Sages' club?" Sloane grinned sheepishly. "Well, quite a few."

"My wonderful disciple, Lochlain Fields, and oh, his mate. There's also his sister, who is also Milo's mate…." Lochlain mumbled a few more names as he counted on his fingers. "Mm. Eight?"

"Ten with Alexander and Rota, plus the vessels Urilith and Galgareth use when they visit Aeon," Sloane added with a grimace. "So, twelve counting me?"

"How the fuck have you guys not been all over the news?" Chase wondered out loud. "Are you passing out flyers?"

"We've really tried to be discreet," Sloane insisted.

"Oh!" Loch suddenly exclaimed. "You must all come by for dinner. Mother and Galgareth are returning soon to help us prepare for the baby. And oh! In your time living as a mortal, have you tried breadsticks yet? The skinny garlic ones that dwell in the freezer?"

"Baby?" Merrick suddenly smiled, gasping in delight. "You have spawned?"

"Unintentionally," Sloane replied, ducking his head with a short laugh.

"Yes." Loch proudly petted Sloane's stomach. "I was very irresponsible."

"Congratulations!" Merrick clapped. "I would be honored to join you and our family for the Neun Monde festivities."

"Wait, someone's pregnant?" Chase asked helplessly.

"I am." Sloane smiled. "If Merrick hasn't already told you, yeah, super fun side effect of copulating with a god. Just make sure he's not thinking about babies in the bedroom and you'll be fine."

"We're not... that's...." Chase couldn't even wrap his mind around the revelation that a man could be pregnant, far too busy trying to keep all the blood in his body from zooming up to his face as he struggled to deny the accusation.

If only it was true....

"We are not a 'thing,' as you so eloquently said earlier," Merrick said firmly.

"He's obviously very attracted to you." Loch quirked a brow. "Why deny yourself? Or is your namesake that important to you?"

"We are partners," Merrick replied as he turned his head away. "Fraternization is forbidden by our code of conduct."

"Oh, but what if you weren't partners?" Loch pressed, his eyes lighting up with excitement.

"That is not important." Merrick began to fidget.

Chase caught the movement immediately—a quick twitch of Merrick's fingers, moving his thumb inward to stroke his palm. It was such a tiny thing, but Chase had only seen Merrick do that when he was nervous.

It was so rare that Chase struggled to think of the last time he'd seen him do it, and he didn't know how to interpret it.

"What is important is now we have cultists to go apprehend and paintings we cannot translate, since the only known speaker of Salgumel's godstongue apparently sacrificed himself to save the world," Merrick declared, and he nodded purposefully to the door. "We need to go."

"Well, thanks for clearing all that up, guys," Chase said with a tip of his hat. "Thanks for not zapping my brain again. Congrats on your god baby." He got up to follow Merrick out. "This has been fun. Educational even. We'll have to do this again real soon."

"Wait, why don't you just ask Ollie?" Sloane scoffed, as if this was plainly obvious.

"Didn't cross my mind." Chase gritted his teeth.

"Who?" Merrick eyed Chase suspiciously.

"Ollie. Oleander Logue," Chase replied with an exasperated sigh. "My nephew."

"The linguist?" Merrick frowned. "He is your nephew? Why did you not say something?"

"Because the last time we saw each other, I fuckin' arrested him."

CHAPTER 4.

BACK IN the car, Merrick sat still as a statue behind the wheel while he patiently waited for Chase to explain himself.

Chase was lighting up a cigarette, imagining various ways to strangle Sloane for bringing up Ollie. Probably not very kind to wish harm upon a pregnant person, but he was pissed. He was already dizzy from the information overload he'd just received, and the throbbing in his head had returned full force.

"So, the linguist who refuses to work for us is my nephew," he began. "My little brother's youngest kid. Was a real good boy for a while until some nasty breakup sent him into crazy land. Started getting into drugs, had some little issues with possession that maybe I helped some people look the other way on. We had a big ol' intervention for him, and he promised to stop."

Merrick was silent, but he nodded.

"I thought he was finally getting better, but a few months ago, he had some sort of relapse." Chase paused to take a drag. "He was at a grocery store and claims he saw a fuckin' monster in there trying to buy garlic. No one else saw shit, and he started freaking out in the parking lot. Got physical with somebody. Cops get called, they call me, and I go down there to try to talk to him.

"He had completely lost it. He was talking crazy about seeing things everywhere, and whoa, big surprise, I find a bunch of damn drugs on him. He refuses to go to rehab or any kinda hospital. I couldn't do him another fuckin' favor, so I arrested him. He spent a few nights in jail, made bail, and well... he ain't spoken to me since.

"Found out he got off with parole since it was his first real offense and heard he quit working for the department. I know it's because of me. My brother's mad at me because I couldn't get his kid outta trouble when all I've been doing is keeping his dumb ass out of it for months."

"You were right to arrest him," Merrick said. "It sounds as if he was taking advantage of your relationship."

"Maybe. Or maybe he's just a stupid kid who really needs help that I couldn't give him." Chase puffed on his cigarette again. "And you know, that's the shitty thing. He's not stupid. I mean, okay, he's a little stupid. Like, I wouldn't leave him in a room by himself for too long with a bunch of sharp objects, but this translating stuff he's been doing? He's great at it."

"He is obviously wasting a great talent."

"Yeah, well, ain't my place to say none of that now. He hates me."

"If he is as skilled as you say, perhaps it is worth visiting him," Merrick suggested. "This is truly a most urgent matter."

"He's not gonna talk to me," Chase grumbled.

"Then I will talk to him," Merrick said firmly. "I will explain how important this is."

"Wiggle your tentacles at him. I'm sure that'll be convincing."

Merrick did not look amused.

"Sorry, fuck, just trying to lighten the mood." Chase sighed, flicking his spent cigarette out the window.

Before Merrick could reprimand him for his cursing or his littering, his phone rang. He made a face at the cracked screen and tried to answer it. "My phone is still not working. It is dispatch."

"Hang on." Chase dug his own phone out of his pocket and dialed the dispatch line. He waited for it to ring before passing it over to Merrick. "Here."

"Thank you."

While Merrick chatted with dispatch, Chase zoned out. He felt terrible about what had happened with Ollie, but he didn't know what else he could have done. Poor kid was seeing monsters everywhere, and that wasn't possible....

Then again, Chase thought, he was currently sitting right next to a god.

"We have a hit on one of the prints from the factory," Merrick said as soon as he got off the phone. "Based on the physical description, I believe it is the man whose face was bandaged. I have instructed them to text message you the address."

"What do you look like?"

"Pardon?" Merrick blinked.

"Like, the real you," Chase clarified. "The god you."

"My godly form is of no consequence," Merrick replied haughtily. "Now, we are going to the residence of Jeffrey Martin. He has a colorful criminal history, and it is rife with theft and unregistered magical assault. He could be—"

"Come on," Chase chided. "You can't look that fuckin' awful. I mean, for fuck's sake, look at me!" He smacked his round belly. "I'm just a few pounds away from a full keg. So tell me. What do you look like?"

"It is irrelevant, your language continues to be too bold, and I do not like you talking about yourself that way," Merrick snapped, his words coming out so quickly it took Chase a few seconds to catch up.

"Okay, wait, wait, but it's totally relevant because I wanna know, fuck your language policing, and why? Why do you fuckin' care?"

"As my partner, you should have nothing but confidence." Merrick fidgeted again as he had in the apartment earlier, cranking the car and hastily exiting the parking lot. "Your self-deprecating humor is unnecessary."

"It's not humor, it's the truth," Chase scolded. "I know what I look like. I'm old, I'm fat, and I'm tired, okay? Whatever I had to offer someone faded a long time ago."

Watching Merrick's fidgeting fingers, Chase was left wondering what the cause was.

Did…. Did Merrick *like* him?

No, that was stupid. Impossible. And yet, it was only when Loch discussed the possibility of them dating that Merrick got so anxious.

Maybe….

"We are here," Merrick announced, parking at the curb and practically leaping out of the car.

Chase followed behind him, and he took a quick look around.

The neighborhood wasn't too shabby, most of the lawns well-groomed, and he saw some kids playing down the street.

Hard to believe a crazy Salgumel worshipper might live here.

Merrick was already at the door, examining the frame with a scowl.

"What's up?" Chase asked. "More wards?"

Curling his fist, Merrick smirked as the top of the door cracked. "Not anymore." He knocked loudly. "AVPD, Mr. Martin! We need to speak with you!"

Merrick took a few steps back, and Chase peered through the windows. There were curtains obscuring his view, but through a tiny sliver he could see…

A body, facedown.

"Merrick," Chase snapped. "Possible vic inside. We gotta get in right now."

Merrick didn't hesitate to strike the door with a quick flick of his tentacle, causing it to slam wide open. Gun drawn, he charged inside.

Chase ran in behind him, getting a glimpse of a sparse living room. He went straight for the body on the floor in front of the couch. He turned it over, grimacing and recoiling immediately. "Ah, for fuck's sake."

"Are they alive?" Merrick demanded, stalking around the perimeter of the foyer and living room.

"No," Chase sighed.

"I did not see you check for a pulse."

"Hard to have a pulse when your heart's been torn out," Chase replied glumly, gesturing to the gaping hole in the dead man's chest.

"That is not Mr. Martin," Merrick observed.

"No, but he's definitely one of the guys who shot at us this morning." Chase made a face. "Guess they came back here to regroup and decided this was a great idea."

"Perhaps it has something to do with the ritual," Merrick mused, wrinkling his nose at the mess. "We need to call this in and get forensics down here as soon as possible."

"Here," Chase said, thrusting his phone at Merrick. He took several steps away from the body and rubbed his forehead. "I need a second."

"Are you all right?" Merrick asked. "Do you need me to call for medical assistance?"

"No, I just feel a little sick." Chase grimaced. "Seeing the inside of somebody's chest ain't doing my stomach any favors."

"Very well." Merrick holstered his weapon and began to dial on Chase's phone. "I will make the call. Take all the time you need."

"I'll go check the rest of the house."

"There is no one else here," Merrick said, his eyes turning black and shining with stars. "Trust me."

"Fine, show-off!" Chase scoffed. "Did your magical little god powers tell you if there's any clues? Yeah, didn't think so!" He stalked off before Merrick could actually reply, desperately wanting space between himself and the corpse.

He headed down a hallway that ran between the living room and the kitchen, and the first door he checked was a bathroom. The second door was a cluttered bedroom that reeked of vomit. Chase moved for the last one, and he stopped.

"Holy fuck."

All the walls were covered in red paint, and strange symbols were scrawled in long, uneven lines. There was an altar in front of the window, cluttered with candles and bowls, and the air was full of a pungent, bitter incense.

Chase cautiously approached the altar, and his stomach tried to visit the back of his throat when he saw what was in the bowls.

Flesh, blood, and a human heart.

That's when he realized the paint on the walls was definitely not paint.

He reeled backward, and he honestly didn't know which room would be worse to stand in. He went back to the vomit bedroom, deciding it was the less volatile of his choices.

There was a dresser, a bed, a trunk, and endless stacks of papers and books strewn across every available horizontal surface.

The papers seemed to be written in gibberish, maybe more of that godstongue crap, and there were literally hundreds of them scattered all around him. A few said things like "ritual," "blood," and "pure," the same words repeating over and over again.

Cheerful.

He opened up the top drawer of the dresser, and he saw a collection of letters. They'd been opened already, and Chase noted they were addressed to their good buddy handprint-face Jeff at the Archersville Penitentiary.

There was no return address, only a doodle of a flower. It was a circle with six little loops for the petals and very simple.

Chase didn't fancy himself an artist, but he thought even he could have done better.

"Forensics is still finishing up over at the factory, but we have some backup coming to help secure the residence," Merrick said, standing in the open doorway. "Found something?"

"Letters," Chase replied, turning back to face Merrick. "Maybe our boy Jeff had a jail-time sweetie." He lifted one of the letters, sniffing. "Yup. Perfume."

"Stop touching things."

"It was one letter!"

"You should not yet disturb the scene."

"The other bedroom is a disturbing scene," Chase declared. "Did you see that shit?"

"Yes," Merrick grumbled, wrinkling his nose. "It looked like a sacrificial ritual, but I cannot say what the intended goal was or if it was achieved."

"Think they're trying that Salgumel wakey thing without having the full set of instructions?"

"Possibly."

"They're like stupid kids trying to figure out sex, and they just keep sticking stuff in their belly buttons," Chase grumbled.

"Excuse me?" Merrick's eyes widened.

"I guarantee they don't know what the full ritual is," Chase said, "so they're just fucking around, trying to make something work."

"I do not understand."

"What? It makes total sense. They must be doing something wrong because we haven't seen any cranky old gods running around trying to take over the world. I bet they got spooked since we broke up their little party, and they're desperate."

"While that is an excellent deduction, I was referring to the belly button metaphor." Merrick cleared his throat awkwardly. "Can you please explain it?"

"Oh! Well, it's not like sex comes naturally to everyone," Chase said, unable to resist the urge to flirt. "I mean, you're a god. I'm sure you didn't have any problems figuring out where to put all those sexy tentacles...."

"I would very much prefer we do not speak of my true identity." Merrick turned his head away, and his fingers began to fidget. "I am also withdrawing my query about the belly button metaphor because I fear it is going to create an opening for a very inappropriate conversation."

"Oh, and we wouldn't want that, would we?" Chase took a few steps closer. "Someone might hear us talking about belly buttons and tentacles and report us for fraternization. Mm, how very scandalous."

"You should not mock our code of conduct like that," Merrick said sternly. "It guides our behavior as officers and helps us maintain a professional partnership."

"Huh, and if we weren't partners?" Chase pushed. He could see Merrick's fingers twitching again. It was a long shot, but if there was any chance that he might feel the same way, Chase had to know.

"Detective Chase," Merrick protested, his jaw tightening.

"You wouldn't tell Loch, but come on." Chase bit his lower lip, edging closer still even as his nerves began to scream at him to retreat. "Tell me."

"I am not going to answer that."

"Why not?"

"Because I do not want to hurt you," Merrick replied, and he looked sad.

I don't want to hurt you when I reject you, is what Chase heard. He smiled through the pain, and he swallowed back a frustrated curse. It was so stupid to ever have gotten his hopes up.

At least now he knew.

"Right," Chase said briskly, looking around for anything to distract himself with. He kneeled down next to the trunk to take a look. "Now, how about we just forget I ever asked."

"Detective Chase—"

"No, no," Chase interrupted, reaching for the latch on the trunk. "Message received, loud and clear."

"Wait! Chase—" Merrick shouted.

Certain he was about to hear direct quotes from their policy-and-procedure manual about this being the best thing for them both, Chase ignored Merrick and flipped open the trunk.

Maybe if he hadn't been so upset, he would have realized Merrick was trying to warn him.

The next sensation Chase felt was heat, followed by a strange prickle of pain. Then he felt arms—whoa, way too many of them—grabbing him and slamming him down on the floor.

Oh, there was the pain again.

Ew, and the smell of burned hair.

"What the fuck?" Chase mumbled, trying to focus his vision and figure out what the hell had just happened.

He was on his back, sprawled out on the floor amidst all the papers, and Merrick was on top of him. His hat was gone, and he was wrapped up in a bunch of clinging tentacles, and Merrick was on top of him. Something had definitely caught on fire, and Merrick....

Nope, not imagining it.

Merrick was absolutely on top of him, and his eyes had turned back into those pretty black pools that took Chase's breath away.

"You idiot!" Merrick bellowed, angrier than Chase had ever seen him.

Well, there Merrick was to fill the awkward silence.

"Do you have any idea what could have happened to you if that fire trap hit you?" Merrick raged on, his hands curling around the lapels of Chase's jacket and giving him a hard shake.

"Crispy Irish bacon?" Chase said stupidly. He grabbed Merrick's wrists to push him away, but he couldn't bring himself to do it. He'd never been in any position nearly this compromising with Merrick before, and he couldn't help how his heart thumped along so quickly.

"You jackass!" Merrick snarled. "You ridiculous, stupid little man!"

"You... cursed!"

"Damn right, I did! You are a *jackass*!"

Chase didn't care what Merrick called him, although the danger of a fire trap was not lost on him.

Fire traps were relatively simple spells with devastating power, and they were commonly used to protect valuables. There was a terrible fire a few years ago that had killed a would-be thief after he tried to open a safe that had been fire trapped, and strict licensing had been put into place to monitor them ever since.

He should have checked the trunk before trying to open it, but he'd been a tiny bit ticked off.

"You could have set this whole place on fire!" Merrick was still going. "This was disgustingly negligent! You are the single most irresponsible human being on this entire plane of existence!"

The fun of being pinned down was losing its novelty now.

"Okay, okay, I fucking get it!" Chase snapped back. "I almost destroyed the fucking evidence! Lay the fuck off, Merry!"

Merrick was startled, and the anger left his face. His expression was now unreadable. "Oh, by Great Azaethoth's horns... you really are stupid."

Chase glared.

"Elwood—"

Wait, did he just say his first name?

"—you could have been killed! You could have died right in front of me! I might...! I might not have been able to... to...." Merrick's handsome face twisted with agony, and he lunged forward and kissed Chase fiercely.

Chase was certain he had actually died in that fire and gone to Zebulon or the Elysian Fields or wherever the hell mostly decent people went. He couldn't believe Merrick was kissing him, and the rush of joy and staggering passion made him gasp.

He was so shocked he couldn't react at first, and his lips were numb as he tried to kiss Merrick back.

All he could think about was that he didn't deserve this man or god or whatever the hell he was. But for this moment, this brief flicker in time, he was going to try and enjoy it.

"I am sorry. I should not have done that!" Merrick tried to pull away. "Please accept my apologies!"

"You only need to apologize if you don't do it again," Chase panted, reaching a hand up to Merrick's hair and dragging him back for another kiss.

Merrick came to him willingly, kissing Chase desperately and running his hands all over his face and through his hair. His legs spread, straddling Chase's hips and pressing him into the floor.

And the tentacles, wow, the tentacles were coiling around Chase's arms and his thighs, and they felt so weirdly new and good and *hot*. He tried reaching up to touch Merrick, but his arms were pinned by the tentacles.

He was able to move his lower body, and he ground up against Merrick's ass with a lusty growl. His cock was diamond-hard, and he groaned when Merrick rocked down against him so very purposefully. He didn't think Merrick's cock was doing anything—wait, did that even work, or was this now just a tentacle thing?—but he definitely seemed to be enjoying himself.

Merrick pulled back, gasping and out of breath, staring down at Chase with starry black eyes. His lips were pink and wet from kissing, and he looked absolutely gorgeous. "Elwood, I did not mean to lose control like that."

"You can lose it any fuckin' time you like," Chase promised, running his tongue over his lips and trying to hold on to the taste of Merrick's kisses.

"We need to stop," Merrick said urgently, "before the nature of my passions betray me again."

"Yeah, I hear what you're saying, but do we really?" Chase wished he could hold him. "I mean, is it really that bad if they get just a tiny bit betrayed?"

"Yes," Merrick insisted. "You do not understand. I have been fighting these desires for months now—"

"Months?" Chase was totally dumbfounded.

"Yes, months!" Merrick confirmed haughtily. "Stop interrupting! I cannot act on my affections for you because I cannot risk jeopardizing the future of Merrick's career!"

"Third-person talk is still so weird!"

"I know my godly essence can easily attract and ensnare the passions of mortals, and that is exactly why I have worked so hard to conceal it!"

"Hold the fuck up!" Chase shook his head, trying to sit up. "You think I'm only hot for you because I found out you're a god?"

"Yes?" Merrick didn't sound so sure now, and he let Chase move up into a sitting position.

"Merrick. Gordoth. Whatever." Chase steadied Merrick in his lap, finally wrapping his arms around him. "Whoever the fuck you are, please hear me out, okay?"

"Elwood," Merrick protested, his hands resting awkwardly on Chase's broad chest. He looked upset, but his tentacles seemed to be hugging Chase closer. "This is unwise."

"I'm crazy about you," Chase said earnestly. "You have no idea. It's been so long, and I—"

There was a knock at the door, and an officer's voice called out, "Detectives?"

"We are in here," Merrick shouted back, quickly hopping off Chase and adjusting his clothes.

Chase watched all of his tentacles slither back out of sight and slumped defeatedly back on the floor.

Merrick was refusing to look at Chase, and his tone was eerily flat when he spoke again. "We are never discussing any of this. None of it. If you do, I will request an immediate transfer and wipe your memory."

"Right." Chase remained on the floor while his heart crumbled. He didn't even have it in him to point out the hypocrisy of threatening to wipe his brain when Merrick had chastised Loch for doing the same thing.

He was too miserable.

"Get up." Merrick glanced out into the hallway, dropping his voice down to a soft hiss. "Get up, they are here."

"I can't."

"Why not?"

"Because my dick is not connected to my heart, and it is currently stuck to my fuckin' thigh. If I stand up, it's gonna be more than a little obvious that—"

"I do not require any additional details!" Merrick jerked his head away. "I will stall them while you handle your anatomy."

"I'll get up in a damn second." Chase had a great joke all lined up about Merrick helping him handle it, but he decided to keep it to himself. He wasn't in the mood anyway.

Once his erection subsided, he retrieved his hat and joined Merrick in the living room with the other officers to help coordinate their efforts. There wasn't much for him to actually do since Merrick was currently in overachiever mode and barking orders left and right.

The scene was secured, and Milo arrived to start cataloging all the evidence. Sloane must have told him the truth about Merrick because Milo kept staring and giving him and Chase a lot of eyebrow waggles and knowing smiles.

Daisy was still back at the lab working on the factory case, and Milo gave them a quick update. It wasn't much, only that they hadn't been able to match any of the other prints, but they might have a lead on one of the paintings.

Apparently, according to Daisy's examination, it was a fake.

Chase tried to stay focused on the work at hand and tell Milo how fascinating all of that was, but he couldn't think clearly.

Merrick liked him too. He liked him a lot if that kiss was anything to go by. But how the hell could he tell Merrick how he really felt if they couldn't talk about it?

He didn't doubt Merrick would follow through on his threats to transfer, but….

"Are you ready?" Merrick asked bluntly.

"What?" Chase blinked out of his stupor.

"Are you ready?" Merrick nodded at the front door. "There is nothing else we can do here, and I want to speak to your nephew."

"Right." Chase cleared his throat. "Can't wait."

Chase gave Merrick directions to where his nephew lived, a modest apartment complex near one of the city's museums. The drive over was deathly silent, and Chase couldn't decide what was fueling his anxiety more, thinking about his kiss with Merrick or having to see Ollie again.

"I will do the talking," Merrick said firmly as they stood in front of Ollie's door.

"Knock yourself out," Chase mumbled, standing off to the side to stay out of the way.

Merrick held his head high and knocked.

Ollie answered the door, his eyes still half-closed as if he had been sleeping. He was only wearing a pair of pajama pants, and his curly red hair was particularly fluffy.

"Hello," Merrick said in his most official voice. "My name is Detective Merrick, and I am here on behalf of the—"

Ollie's eyes suddenly bugged out, and he screamed. It was a blood-curdling screech, a sound of absolute terror, and he slammed the door right in Merrick's face.

"Huh."

"Yeah," Chase quipped, "that went well."

CHAPTER 5.

"WHAT IS wrong with him?" Merrick wondered out loud. "Is it the drugs?"

"Who the fuck knows," Chase grunted, joining Merrick at the door and knocking impatiently. "Hey, Ollie! It's me! Uncle Elwood! Open the fuck up, kid!"

"Uncle Elwood?" Ollie shouted back, sounding alarmed. "No fuckin' way! You and your freaky-ass buddy need to go away! Like, just, just go right now!"

"Ollie, please—"

"He has *tentacles*! No!"

Merrick and Chase stared at each other.

"He can see me," Merrick whispered hurriedly.

"Fucking how?" Chase spat back. "How is that possible?"

"He must be blessed by the gods."

"Oh, right, that totally explains it." Chase knocked again, raising his voice again as he pleaded, "Ollie, we just wanna talk, okay? Please?"

"No! I'm still not talking to you!" Ollie growled.

"Technically, you're talking to me right now," Chase pointed out. "Look, we need your help. I'm not even being dramatic when I say the fate of the fuckin' world is at stake here."

The door opened a tiny crack, and Ollie peered at them suspiciously. "Really?"

"Yes," Chase promised.

Ollie cut his eyes at Merrick. "Do you see it?"

"See what?"

"What he is," Ollie said. "That thing inside of him."

"Well, I can't see it right now, but I know it's there."

Ollie's eyes widened, and he opened the door a little more. "You believe me now?"

Chase thought back to all the other times Ollie had claimed he'd seen monsters, and his heart clenched. Maybe he'd been wrong about Ollie and his visions, and he wanted to make this right.

"Yes," he confirmed, "and I owe you a real big fuckin' apology." He offered a sympathetic smile. "Can we come in?"

"I… I guess." Ollie slowly opened the door, backpedaling a safe distance away.

Ollie went in first with Merrick right behind him, and he took a quick glance around the apartment.

It was packed full of plants, crystals, wicker furniture, and it reeked of incense and old booze. The trash peeking out from the kitchen was full, and a few empty bottles of alcohol were clustered around it. There were charms hanging in the windows, wind chimes with colored bits of glass, shining Sagittarian totems, and tight bundles of dried flowers.

"We require your assistance," Merrick began in that firm voice of his once the door was shut behind them.

"No, no, me first." Ollie hugged himself, defiantly staring down Merrick. "You. What are you? You're all squished up in there, but I can see you."

"I am Gordoth the Untouched," Merrick replied, "brother of Salgumel, Shartorath, Yeris, Ulgon, Elgrirath, Zarnorach, Xarbon, Solmach, Eb, Ebb, Ebbeth, and Lozathin. I was spawned by Baub, the child of Zunnerath and Halandrach, they who were born of Etheril and Xarapharos, descended directly from Great Azaethoth himself."

"Justice," Ollie said, his jaw hanging wide open. "You're the god of justice."

"Yes. Now, how are you doing this?" Merrick asked. He took a few steps toward Ollie, his bright eyes turning black. "How can you see me?"

"Whoa, whoa!" Ollie cried out. "Back off, Wiggles!"

"I mean you no harm, mortal child," Merrick soothed, offering his hand and a few tentacles as he continued to advance. "Please."

"No! Nope! No touchie! Get up out of my personal space!" Ollie held up his finger to keep Merrick away. "I'll tell you whatever you want to know. Just cool it with the squiggly bits!"

"How about we sit down, huh?" Chase nudged Merrick. "And put said squiggly bits away, huh?"

Merrick actually looked insulted, but he withdrew to the sofa. His tentacles went back inside his sleeve, and he tucked his hands in his lap. He had the demeanor of a puppy whose nose had just been bopped with a newspaper.

"So, uh, right, I maybe have starsight?" Ollie said, scooting into the kitchen. He returned with a bottle of vodka and tipped it back.

"The fuck?" Chase asked, reaching over to take the bottle so Ollie would stop chugging. "Like, psychic powers? Divine magic? Need a Class S license for magic like that, and I know you ain't got one."

"Exactly," Ollie snapped. "Which is why I never told anybody. Especially you, by the way."

Chase ignored how that hurt and took a drink from the bottle before handing it back. He gave Merrick a warning look, and thankfully no verbal reprimands came about drinking while on the clock.

"Was this a congenital blessing?" Merrick asked politely.

"No, my parents were married, you jerk," Ollie replied with a short huff. "It happened after my ex-boyfriend died."

Merrick stared.

"Congenital means 'since birth,' kiddo," Chase explained patiently.

"Oh… well." Ollie scowled. "I knew that!"

"Now, what boyfriend?" Chase sat down on the sofa next to Merrick. "You haven't seen anybody since you broke up with that big guy who worked at the funeral home. I mean, that's kinda when you started going downhill."

"Ted," Ollie supplied, smiling sadly as he raised the bottle back up. "That's the one. That's how it all started."

"I'm sorry, I thought you guys just broke up. I didn't know he died."

"Well, that's because I brought him back to life."

"Necromancy?" Chase's eyes widened. "Are you fuckin' kidding me, kid?"

"It is a serious felony," Merrick cautioned, "and true necromancy hasn't been seen in hundreds of years. That is both a very bold and very foolish claim to make."

"Says the wiggly god guy who's supposed to be in sleepy land," Ollie scoffed. "Anything's possible, squid dude."

"Look, just talk to me. Tell me what happened," Chase urged, trying to keep Ollie's attention. "No offense, kid, but you really expect me to believe you were able to bring someone back from the dead?"

"What the fuck is that supposed to mean?" Ollie demanded.

"You've been doing real great with this translating gig, I'll give you that, but...."

"But what?"

"Ollie," Chase said cautiously, "you asked me where all the stars go during the daytime."

"Oh, come on." Ollie's face turned red. "I was probably, like, you know, really young—"

"This was last year at your mother's birthday. And speaking of your mom, when you wanted to make her cookies for Mother's Day, you bought two 'M' cookie cutters."

"Because there's two m's in the word mom," Ollie mumbled defiantly. "Duh."

"Kiddo, you tried to take toast out of a toaster with a fork."

"Well, how else was I supposed to get it out? The lifty pusher-up thing was stuck!" Ollie turned up his nose. "I don't like what you're implicating here, Uncle."

"Oleander," Chase said with all the sincerity he could muster, "you are one of the sweetest kids I know, but come on. I feel like necromancy is a tiny bit out of your league."

"Let him speak," Merrick said suddenly. He looked to Ollie. "You say that you were able to resurrect your lover. Tell us how you did it."

"Sure thing, Wiggles," Ollie said as he flopped down in a worn wicker chair beside them. He gave Chase a dirty look before clearing his throat and saying, "I loved Ted more than anything. He was it for me. We had gone to the beach for the weekend, and I proposed... which apparently was the totally wrong thing to do.

"Ted got super mad at me, said he wasn't ready, and we got in a huge fight. Then, well, he might have maybe drowned trying to save this boy. His name was Graham. Super sweet little guy, and he thought Ted was so cool. Asked him if he was part giant and all this cute shit, and he really wanted him to take him out into the waves.

"He came over to talk to Ted about it right after our big fight, and well, Ted snapped at him. Really upset him, and the poor little guy ran away crying. Ted cools down and gets to bitching about finding some sunscreen, and that's when we heard Graham's mom start screaming. Since Ted wouldn't take him into the water, Graham went by himself."

"Fuck," Chase whispered, hating that he could already see where the story was headed.

It was nowhere good.

"Ted went after him, and he never came back up," Ollie went on, his voice now flat, as if trying to separate himself from what was obviously a painful memory. "They got their bodies, dragged 'em up on the beach. Paramedics show up, and they even got some fancy healer who was there vacationing with his family. They were all trying to save little Graham, and I ran over to Ted.

"He was dead. I mean, I know he was dead. Everyone had given up on him and was trying to save the kid. And I was so angry, so fuckin' angry. I don't know exactly what happened. I remember shaking him and wishing that I knew what to do." He smiled bitterly. "That for once in my life I wouldn't be stupid ol' Ollie, and I would know what the big magical secret was to bring him back."

Chase cringed, knowing he had more than contributed to Ollie's doubts about his intelligence—especially just in this conversation.

"And you got it." Merrick nodded in understanding. "You received the sight to see all that is unseen."

"Yeah, that." Ollie leaned back in his chair, and the wicker creaked. "I could see it. The words just popped up in my head, and I knew exactly what to do and what it was gonna cost me."

"You knew?" Merrick frowned. "And you still did it?"

"I loved him," Ollie said, shrugging as he took another drink. "It didn't matter."

"What happened to the boy?" Chase asked hesitantly.

"I wanted to save him too," Ollie replied, his brow furrowing up. "I really did, but the ambulance took him away before I could. I mean, I don't even know if I could have done it twice because of the cost, but I woulda tried."

"The cost is what? Life?"

"Yup." Ollie touched his bare chest. "Part of my heart will always be with Ted Sturm, quite literally."

"Wait, wait." Chase fumbled for a cigarette. He saw Ollie eyeballing them and offered him one. "So, you get this crazy magic blessing, bring your would-be fiancé back from the dead, and you still break up?"

"When he woke up, he didn't remember what had happened," Ollie replied, nodding in gratitude as he took the cigarette and grabbed a lighter from the coffee table to light up. "Not the kid, not dying, nothing. He was still being a dick, and yeah, the ride home wasn't real great. He dumped me, and I never told him the truth."

"But why the fuck not?" Chase asked, sparking a fire with his fingers to light his cigarette. "He owes you his life!"

"That's not a real reason to stay with somebody," Ollie protested. "I wouldn't want Ted to be with me because he felt like he owes me something. I wanted him to be with me because he loved me." He flicked his cigarette in the general direction of the ashtray. "So I let him go."

"And then what?" Merrick pressed. "Your starsight abilities continued to grow, yes?"

"Yeah," Ollie said. "Started seeing shit I didn't understand all the time. Some people look normal enough, but then they're all black and rotten inside. I once saw a guy who looked like an angel, but underneath his skin was nothing but death. Plus, I could suddenly read all the Japanese on my pocky and my mochi cakes."

"And the monster at the grocery store?"

"Some crazy wiggly thing all crammed into a body like him," Ollie said, pointing at Merrick. "I had never seen anything like it before."

"Was this guy a redhead?" Chase asked slowly.

"Yeah, why?"

"I think that may have been Azaethoth," Chase replied, glancing at Merrick. "The night he zapped my brain, he was screaming about garlic and stole a fake tree from a grocery store. I woke up at home with no clue how I got there, and that's when I got the call about Ollie freaking out at what I bet was the same grocery store."

"You know that other wiggly guy?" Ollie demanded, scowling at Merrick. "Well, you tell him he's a giant jerk, and I hope whatever he was making with that garlic was awful. He's the damn reason I got arrested!"

"That's why you started getting into drugs?" Chase asked cautiously. "All the shit you were seeing?"

"Was trying to find a way to make it stop," Ollie said with a grimace. "Spoiler alert, it doesn't work." He gestured to the bottle in his hand. "This doesn't really help either, but at least I can sleep."

"I'm sorry," Chase said, and he hated it because it didn't sound like it was enough. His neglected cigarette had become one long cylindrical ash, and he dropped it into the ashtray to smother what was left.

Ollie shook his head in reply, looking down at his bottle.

"No, Oleander, I'm sorry," Chase said again more earnestly. "All this time, I thought you were crazy. I thought it was the drugs—"

"Just stop," Ollie protested.

"No, I'm sorry." Chase reached out to touch his knee and squeeze it. His heart felt heavy, and he had to get this out. "I fucked up, okay? I should have believed you. I can't go back and fix it, but I can help you now. Whatever you need."

"Uncle Elwood, there's nothing you can do to help me," Ollie insisted. "The drinking isn't great, I know, but I've been clean since I got arrested. I swear. I've got it all handled now."

"What if we get you registered?" Chase offered, patting Ollie's leg. "I know there's programs out there for people who got powers like this."

"Ha!" Ollie jerked away. "Not fuckin' happening. You can't tell anybody. Not ever."

"Using an ability of this magnitude requires a Class S license," Merrick said. "Operating without one makes you a rogue witch. Do you understand that?"

"Yeah, and what kinda license do you gotta have for all them tentacles, huh?" Ollie shot back. "I am not getting registered. I know what happens to people with Class S licenses. The government makes them all go bye-bye, and they take them to a secret lab like they did with Fish Boy!"

"Fish Boy?" Chase snorted. "That fake-ass thing from the tabloids? Ollie, no. That's not true!"

"No. I'm not doing it. No fuckin' way." Ollie narrowed his eyes. "You guys came here 'cause you needed my help, right? If you want me to help you, then you're not gonna say a word about this to anybody."

"You seriously haven't told anybody else?"

"Nope. Not my parents, not my sister, not a damn soul. I've been perfectly happy right here in my own little world, trying not to go crazy all by myself. The only thing I need from you is to pretty please not arrest me."

"I want you to get help, kiddo." Chase waved at the bottle. "Not drink yourself to death."

"You wanna help me, you can leave me alone. I'll do whatever it is you want with the added bonus of not telling everybody ever that an old god is working at the AVPD."

"You would blackmail us?" Merrick demanded.

"Yup." Ollie grinned. "I sure would. Not very fair of me, I know that kinda thing is real important to you, O' Wiggles of justice, but I'm sure you understand. I don't wanna go to jail, and I bet you wanna save the world or whatever it is, right?"

"Damn. Didn't think you had it in you, kid." Chase was actually proud. "Good for you."

"Who's stupid now?" Ollie mumbled triumphantly through a sip of vodka.

"We could still arrest him," Merrick mused out loud. "Practicing Class S magic without a license, failure to register newly developed magical skills, conveying threats to an officer."

"Merrick," Chase grunted. "Let it go. We need him. Saving the world trumps your mortal officer duties, remember?" He looked to Ollie. "This starsight thing, is that how you translate stuff?"

"Yeah," Ollie replied. "I look at the words, and well, I read them. Like, I just see it, whatever it is."

"We got some ancient-ass paintings that we need you to look at," Chase explained. "They contain some kind of ritual that's supposed to wake up Salgumel. You know who he is, right?"

"God of dreams and sleep. Wow. No, that's bad." Ollie appeared to be sobering up at the thought. "That's, like, super bad."

"Yeah. We were hoping there's something in these paintings that might help us figure out how to find these jerkoffs."

"Fine. Just lemme see them."

"We can bring you photographs. That work?"

"Yeah." Ollie stood up, frowning at Merrick and Chase. "You really think this ritual can wake up Salgumel?"

"We do," Merrick replied. "It is imperative we find these wicked men and stop them as soon as possible."

"I'll do whatever I can to help," Ollie promised.

"Thank you," Chase said. "I'll call in and get the pics, and then I'll send them over to you." He paused. "Maybe I could come by and hang out? Help you go through them?"

"No thanks," Ollie replied. "I work better alone. Send me the pics and I'll get you the translations, okay?" He glanced between them, making a bit of a face at Merrick. "Anything else?"

Chase could tell from Ollie's tone that he wanted them to leave. "No, uh, that's it." He stood up, nodding for Merrick to follow. "You take care of yourself, kiddo. Call me if you need anything. I mean, even if you just wanna talk—"

"I'm good, Uncle Elwood," Ollie cut in sharply, and he looked away. "Thanks."

Chase chose not to comment on how that was the most insincere "thanks" ever uttered, and he left without another word. He vaguely heard Merrick bidding Ollie farewell, but he didn't stick around to hear what was said.

He was already lighting another cigarette back at the car by the time Merrick had caught up, and he said, "So, he translates the paintings, and we hope we learn something useful."

"You are hurting," Merrick said.

"I'm fine."

"How many cigarettes have you had?"

"Today's been a shitty day, okay?" Chase took a long drag from his cigarette. "All this time, my nephew has been going nuts seeing some very fucked-up shit. And when he tried to tell me, I just thought he was high. Oh, and I arrested him."

"You cannot hold yourself responsible. He was not being honest with you."

"I should have known something was up when he started cracking all those crazy codes for the department and speaking fuckin' *Klingon*. He almost failed English class in high school. Twice. I thought maybe he'd finally found his niche or whatever."

"You cannot change what's already been done," Merrick said. "You can only control what you do moving forward. If Ollie does not wish to make amends yet, you must not try to force it."

"Look, I appreciate you're trying to have this tender moment with me, but please don't."

"Have I offended you?" Merrick asked, looking genuinely concerned.

"Oh, not at all," Chase said sarcastically. He took out his phone to call the department, mimicking Merrick under his breath, "Have I offended you? Oh, have I?"

"That is extremely rude," Merrick griped.

Chase ignored him and punched in the extension for the forensics lab.

"Forensics, this is Milo," Milo answered, "where you too can be part of the solution and not the precipitate."

"Hey, Milo," Chase greeted. "I need you to send me some photos of those old paintings from the factory."

Merrick got in the car and cranked the engine. Chase saw the brake lights illuminate, and he actually thought for a moment Merrick might leave him there. He flicked away his cigarette and hopped in the passenger seat.

"Yeah, I can email them to you," Milo was saying. "That work?"

"Sure thing."

"I just got back from that homicide, and we've got, like, a million years' worth of evidence to process, but Daisy got a lead on those paintings."

"Oh?" Chase switched the phone to speaker mode so Merrick could hear as well. "Go on, Merrick is here too."

"I'm listening," Merrick said, pulling out of the parking space and heading back to the street. "You have something for us, Milo?"

"Yup! Fun and exciting news!" Milo said. "We found the owner of the fake painting."

"Okay." Chase paused. "And this is relevant because?"

"The owner is a guy named Slappy Romero—"

"Slappy? What kinda name is Slappy?"

"Look, I'm not his mother. I didn't do it. Just listen for a second. Mr. Romero—"

"Slappy."

"Yes, Slappy." Milo huffed. "He's done time for fraud and counterfeiting, so he's a shady dude when he's not being a super smooth art dealer. He got a big payday from his insurance company a few years ago when *The Moist Fertility of Urilitha's Nethers* was stolen.

"Very heartbreaking loss, was the crown jewel of his collection. And wouldn't you know it? He applied for another insurance payout for the painting being stolen earlier this year from his gallery."

"Wait," Merrick said, frowning. "He's had the same painting stolen twice?"

"Different insurance company, same painting," Milo replied. "What's super fun is that both insurance companies sent out appraisers to examine the painting both times to ensure its authenticity."

"And it was legit?" Chase asked.

"Both times."

"So, he's what? Keeping the real painting and making bank by having a bunch of fake copies stolen?"

"How should I know? You guys are the detectives. Go detect! I'm sending you his home address, and then I'll get those pictures over."

"Thanks, Milo."

"Good luck, guys!"

Chase hung up the phone with a sigh. "This is a damn stretch. Chasin' some crooked-ass art collector when we should be looking for our rotten ol' buddy Jeff."

"I would offer some suggestions, but I fear I may offend you," Merrick said coldly, staring straight out the window.

"Oh, don't you start," Chase complained. "If anyone has a reason to be butthurt today, it's me."

"You?" Merrick scoffed, gripping the steering wheel tightly as he made a quick right turn.

"Yes, me!" Chase argued, scowling as he had to brace himself against the passenger door.

"You are being very inconsiderate of my feelings."

"Me? Being inconsiderate of *your* feelings?" Chase sneered. "Ha!"

"You are not the only one who is hurting!"

"Oh, stuff a sock in it, your godliness!"

"Stuff what where now?" Merrick's anger gave way to bewilderment.

"A fuckin' sock!" Chase shouted. "Take a fuckin' sock and stuff it right up your—"

He never got to finish the sentence as the car was suddenly engulfed in flames. It happened so fast that Chase didn't understand what was going on until it was too late. He couldn't breathe through the thick and noxious smoke, and he felt horrible pain all over his body as the car crashed into something and came to a sudden stop.

His final thought was that he couldn't believe his last words were going to be telling a god he loved to do awful things with a sock.

CHAPTER 6.

"ELWOOD?" MERRICK'S voice was pleading desperately. "Please wake up. Please. You need to wake up."

"Huh…?" Chase's vision was fuzzy, and his entire body was aching. He wasn't in the car, he realized. He was on his back with his head in Merrick's lap. He had no idea where his hat was. They were over on the sidewalk, and he could hear sirens wailing in the distance.

He could still smell smoke, and he could hear the crackle of flames popping nearby. He was trying to put together what had happened when he remembered the ball of fire swallowing them up.

Oh, and what he'd said to Merrick about where to put that sock.

"Do you trust me?" Merrick asked hurriedly.

"Right now, strong maybe," Chase mumbled. "What?"

"I need for you to drink some of my seed," Merrick said, looking quite distressed. "I was not able to get us out of the car in time, and you have been very severely hurt. I am trying to heal you, and my seed is quite potent. It will help."

"Your… what?" Chase could feel the tickle of a tentacle beneath his shirt, and he could sense that the only thing keeping him from sheer agony was Merrick's godly touch. "Seed?"

"Yes. Please hurry," Merrick said urgently. "I want to heal you, but this will be a great risk. I may unintentionally reveal myself."

"Yes, seed, whatever." Chase groaned as some of the pain slipped through and made his entire chest throb. "Just do it."

"Brace yourself." Merrick pressed his hand to the side of Chase's face, and a tentacle peeked out from his sleeve.

It was thicker than the others Chase had seen, and there was a small slit at the end. It brushed over Chase's lips, and he instinctively opened his mouth. He gasped in surprise as the tentacle pushed right inside, and he could taste *something*—a fluid, sweet and thick—and he swallowed.

The following warmth was hard to describe, but it was similar to dipping into a hot bath or getting a really big hug. Chase felt safe, comforted, and the pain was fading. As he felt better, his thoughts cleared, and he realized he was sucking on Merrick's tentacle.

Merrick's expression was soft, almost reverent, and the obvious sexual implication of what they were doing was not lost on Chase. His face was getting hot, and he couldn't help how his tongue stroked the underside of the tentacle.

For a few precious seconds, he could pretend this wasn't some very bizarre lifesaving act.

"Elwood," Merrick breathed. His lashes began to flutter. "That is…. You…. You should not do that. You need to rest."

Chase sucked as hard as he could.

"Oh!" Merrick gasped, and his eyes widened.

Chase nearly choked as his mouth was flooded with another hot load.

"Elwood!" Merrick was immediately flustered, and the tentacle quickly slithered back down his sleeve. "Are you all right?"

"Mmm." After licking his lips, Chase grinned sheepishly. "Sorry. I didn't mean, uh, to do whatever it is I did."

"It is okay," Merrick said, though he still seemed worked up. He wiped off his brow and cleared his throat loudly. "I was not expecting that. My apologies. I was… I was not trying to give you so much."

"Well, it worked," Chase said, groaning as he sat up. The pain was but a memory now, and he honestly couldn't remember the last time he'd felt this refreshed. "Damn good stuff you got there."

Merrick looked embarrassed and ducked his head.

Today's level of weirdness had to be maxed out after almost dying in a flaming car and being saved by a tentacle god's magical come.

Then again, the day wasn't over yet.

Chase watched the car burn, and he struggled to think of something else to say. No matter the reason, he had never expected to get this intimate with Merrick, and he didn't know how to handle the sudden onslaught of emotions.

He wanted to kiss him again, fall into his arms, and beg for a thousand other wonderful things he didn't have the right to ask for.

Being alive had to be enough.

Chase reached up for his hat and found nothing, certain now the car had claimed it. His clothes weren't much better off.

"Here." Merrick offered a very familiar though slightly singed fedora. "I know you are fond of it." He glanced at Chase's burned clothing, and the worst of the damage repaired itself. "I am afraid full restoration would be too suspicious, but I hope the state of your hat is acceptable."

"Thanks." Chase put it on and leaned his head back. "It looks great. Gives it some character." He leaned too far and nearly fell over. "So, the fuck happened?"

Merrick reached out to steady him as he replied, "It was another fire trap. This one was set on a timer, and it was cast on the fuel tank of my vehicle."

"What the fuck?"

"Someone must have followed us from the factory or Mr. Jeffrey Martin's house."

"Shit." Chase narrowed his eyes. "Hey, you can't blame this one on me."

"I am not. I am only blaming myself. I have been distracted, and I should have sensed something was wrong." Merrick hung his head. "I nearly got you killed."

"It's not your fault," Chase scoffed. "Come on. Who the fuck puts a damn fire trap on a fuel tank?"

"I believe it was Mr. Martin," Merrick said with a scowl. "There is something rotten in him, and I was able to detect its lingering foul presence on the vehicle." He cringed. "Before it was totally consumed in flames, that is."

"Sidebar here, but, uh, he's not a ghoul?"

"No. Something is eating at him, and he is using very strong magic to keep it at bay." Merrick's brow furrowed in that very endearing way Chase adored so much. "Ghouls smell like a dead body rotting. This... this is like a living person rotting. I have never seen such magic before."

"Goody."

The first fire truck was pulling up now to tend to the flaming car, and several squad cars were right behind it. The streets had mostly cleared already, and officers were quickly dispersing to move anyone left safely out of the way.

"Now you are going to get screened by the medics, and we are returning home to rest," Merrick said firmly.

"We?"

"It is entirely plausible Mr. Martin and his companions are targeting us now. I am not leaving you unguarded until they are apprehended."

"Uh...." Chase's brain went offline when he tried to come up with all the different reasons why that was a terrible idea, and his traitorous tongue replied, "Sure."

"The captain is going to send both of us home for the day," Merrick said glumly, "but we should be able to continue working at your place. You have the internet, yes?"

"And food," Chase replied dumbly. "I, I could cook for you."

"Unnecessary, and you need to focus on resting your mortal body," Merrick retorted, looking up as their fellow officers and paramedics swarmed toward them. "Here we go."

"Yup."

They were both given oxygen and had their vitals taken repeatedly to ensure they were well. Chase explained Merrick had smelled the smoke and was able to get them out of the car before it caught on fire, and everyone seemed to buy that story.

Chase and Merrick both declined a hospital trip, and as expected, their captain sent them both home for the day. The search for Jeffrey Martin was going to be intensified, and now every officer in the city would know his face.

After all, he'd tried to kill two cops.

Easy way to become very popular.

When it was all over, one of their fellow officers offered to give them a ride back to the station.

"You can take us to Detective Chase's residence," Merrick said firmly. "We will make arrangements for transportation to return to the department in the morning."

Chase didn't miss how the officer eyed them, and he turned his head to stare out the window to avoid any incriminating expressions.

After all, he would have given certain parts of his body for this sort of arrangement under different circumstances, and he was worried his face would give it away.

They thanked the officer for the ride, and Chase hated how apprehensive he felt about Merrick seeing his apartment. He knew he definitely had not left it this morning in any sort of shape for company.

"Don't mind the mess," Chase said when he opened the door. "Like, in fact, don't even look at it. Just close your eyes."

"Come on," Merrick snorted as he stepped in behind him. "It really cannot be…." He paused.

The apartment was an absolute disaster. There were several takeout containers and pizza boxes in a haphazard heap in the kitchen, cluttering up the counters, and an impressive beer bottle collection covered both the dining room table and the coffee table in the living room.

"My maid took the week off." Chase took off his slightly scorched hat and jacket and then stepped into the kitchen to make a drink. He usually stuck to beer or the occasional box of wine, but tonight called for something much stronger.

"Chase." Merrick followed him, watching him pour a glass of scotch with a disapproving scowl. "First of all, it is too early in the day for alcohol. Secondly, I am very concerned about the sanitation here, or should I say the lack thereof."

"I was almost set on fire twice today. I'm having a drink, and I'll get a damn trash bag in a second." Chase resisted the urge to tip the bottle up. It made him think of Ollie, and he patted his pockets for his phone. He had several new text messages. "Ollie's started on the translation."

"Yes?" Merrick perked up. "What does it say?"

Chase read the message twice to make sure he wasn't imagining it. He took a sip of his drink. And another. And one more. Nope, still wasn't gonna read *this* out loud to Merrick, especially after whatever the hell they'd done with his tentacle earlier.

"Well?"

Chase offered his phone.

Merrick looked annoyed, but he took it so he could read. His eyes scanned the text and widened, and he said, "Oh!"

"Uh-huh." Chase leaned against the counter, watching Merrick read. "Looks like this Collins guy was a bit freaky, huh? I'm not an expert or anything, but 'his pulsating meaty shaft' ain't part of any magical ritual I've ever heard of."

"Not that it matters, but there are many rituals that involve sex," Merrick mumbled as he handed the phone back. "There is great power in coupling."

"Is that what happened earlier on the sidewalk? Did we 'couple'?"

"I did not mean for the act to become so sexual," Merrick protested, getting flustered again. "As a god, it is quite natural for us to share our seed as a blessing to our worshippers. I prefer to pass it on in a bowl instead of gifting it directly."

"Kinky."

"No, it is not!" Merrick planted his hands on his hips and glared. "You are the one whose gutter mind is perverting a sacred rite."

"Spreading your seed around like that is sacred?" Chase laughed, taking another drink. "How do you not have, like, a zillion kids running around?"

"Our reproduction does not work that way."

Chase hated how very much interested he was in all of that, but he resisted the urge to ask. He was in enough trouble just having Merrick there.

"Perhaps we should tell Oleander to skip that particular painting?" Merrick suggested, eager to change the subject.

"And miss the chance to watch you squirm while you read about 'moist channels'? Never."

Merrick made a face.

Laughing to himself, Chase began to bag up the trash. As he reached for a pizza box, the entire mess vanished. He looked around to find a neat row of trash bags lined up by the front door, and all of the garbage had been whisked away.

He hadn't heard or seen any sign of Merrick casting a spell, and he was extremely impressed.

"Wow. Uh... thanks."

"My pleasure."

"Did you leave a lemony scent too?"

"I wanted to help," Merrick said. "Besides, we have more important things to be worried about than your cleanliness."

"Ah, well, I appreciate it." Chase headed over to the sofa. He noted Merrick's godly powers had even extended down to the crumbs between the cushions. "Think you'd be willing to come by, like, once a week and do all that?"

"No," Merrick replied with a wrinkle of his nose. "Now, when we see Mr. Romero tomorrow, we should arrive first thing to catch him off guard. If he has been producing fakes of the original painting to pass off for his scams, perhaps he knows how valuable the original is."

"You mean that he knows there's part of a ritual or some sexy stuff hidden behind the paint?"

"Precisely," Merrick said, primly sitting down next to Chase. He looked up at the ceiling as he asked, "How are you feeling now? Well, I hope?"

"Definitely better than I have in a long time," Chase replied. "Thanks for saving my life again."

"And for cleaning your apartment."

"Hey, I was gonna get around to the apartment eventually." Chase smirked. "You didn't have to do all that."

"Yes, actually, I did—"

"Just had to get a peek at all my stuff, huh?" Chase teased. "Did you have fun looking around in the bedroom? Sorry to disappoint you, but my leather pants and ball gags are at the cleaners."

"It is moments like these when I am not sure if you are joking or not, and I have no idea how to respond." Merrick's lips tugged up in a small smile. "I did not go into your bedroom."

"Scared?"

"After seeing the rest of the apartment, I had legitimate reasons to be concerned."

Chase laughed, and he was happy to see Merrick smile. "I'll have you know that's the cleanest room in this place. Don't even waste your time in there."

"Waste?" Merrick grinned.

"Yeah, you heard me. I've always tried to be a garbage can kinda guy, not a garbage can't, and I like coming home to a clean bed, thank you."

Now Merrick was laughing, and he teased, "Ah, heh, so the bed is clean, but what about the floor?"

"Just don't ever look down. Problem solved!"

Merrick laughed again, and he actually seemed to relax. He leaned into the sofa, and Chase could see the tension leaving his shoulders.

"Hey, what has four wheels and flies?"

"What?"

"A garbage truck!"

Merrick snickered. "Oh, that is terrible!"

"Bah, you love it," Chase said proudly. "I've now officially run through all three trash jokes I know, so don't be expecting a big finish or anything."

"I am quite satisfied. Thank you."

"Mmm." Chase sipped his scotch. He wasn't sure what to say now, and the day's many turbulent events left him feeling unsettled.

"What is it?" Merrick asked.

"Long-ass day." Chase shrugged. "Somewhere in between the fire traps and dead bodies and finding out you're a god…." He paused, unable to finish the thought. "Sorry."

"Is this about the sock placement you referred to earlier?" Merrick frowned.

Cringing, Chase confirmed, "Ah, that's definitely part of it."

"I am sorry you have been hurt today," Merrick said quietly, his body beginning to tighten up again. "I know my actions are responsible for some of it, but that was never my intention."

"I'm sorry too." Chase finished off his drink. "I wasn't trying to piss you off either. It's not every day you find out—" *The man of your dreams.* "—the guy you work with is a god, you know."

"I am well aware." Merrick hung his head. "I do not like it has changed us so much in one day. Your newfound affection for me is very flattering, but it is an undesired side effect."

"Don't you start that shit again," Chase warned.

"What 'shit' is that, Chase?" Merrick countered. "Is it too much to want someone to desire me without having to reveal I am a god first?" He looked away, sullen and hurt. "Forget it. I said we weren't going to discuss it, and here I am—"

"Oh no. We're definitely talkin' about it now, and you can take all your little threats about being transferred and shove 'em right up there with the sock."

"Detective Chase!" Merrick gasped. "You cannot!"

"No." Chase slammed the empty glass down and turned to face Merrick. "I'm not listening to this whole 'wah, you only like me 'cause I'm a god' bullshit for another second."

"Detective—" Merrick's brow furrowed up in anger.

"I'm in love with you," Chase said firmly, watching Merrick's rage fade into complete shock. He was determined to get this out, all of it, and finally tell Merrick how he felt. He reached for his hand and gave it a small squeeze. "Did you hear me?"

"Yes?" Merrick sounded confused, but he hadn't pulled away.

"I've been in love with you for so long, I really don't think I can't *not* love you," Chase went on. "I say stupid stuff and flirt and invite you over for no-pants time because I'm a big idiot, and I have no idea how to tell you how incredible I think you are. I wanted you way before I ever knew you were a fuckin' god, and I mean, let's face it. You were always like a god to me anyway, 'cause all I ever wanted to do was worship you.

"Just being near you was enough for me, just… just being able to work with you, to get to know you. I don't care if you don't wanna have any physical pleasures or whatever with me. I don't care if you don't ever wanna speak to me again and decide to get that transfer. But don't you dare question how I feel about you after you made a bunch of crappy assumptions. I love you. You're an idiot, but I still love you."

"Elwood," Merrick murmured, his eyes getting dark. His fingers awkwardly twined with Chase's, and he was starting to breathe faster. "You… you truly mean all of that? All those wonderful things?"

"Yeah," Chase said as he gulped back a wave of nerves. "Almost dying for the second time today has kinda lit a fire under my ass, I guess. Or maybe it was the third time. I've lost count. I just... I just can't listen to you say that crap. Maybe you got it with mortals only wanting you 'cause you're a god. I get it. But that's not me."

"You are really in love with me?" Merrick still sounded as if he couldn't quite believe it.

"Some great detective you are," Chase teased lightly. "Kinda been this way for a while."

"I suspected that you desired me physically after the invitation of no pants, but I truly had no idea your feelings carried this depth."

"Why else do you think I put up with your crap?"

"I must also confess my affections for you. I have had the most impure thoughts about you—"

"Me?"

"Yes," Merrick replied earnestly. "And just as you do not want to hear me complain about my godly attributes preventing me from finding true passion, I do not want to hear you speak poorly of yourself."

"I'm almost twice your age," Chase said weakly. "I mean... come on."

"Are you now?" Merrick smiled, and he looked downright sly. "I do believe I am much older than you."

"Only by a few thousand years." Chase laughed at the truth of it. "Damn cradle robber."

"Huh?"

"Don't ask. Right. Forget I said anything."

"Even after all these years, I still find myself struggling with some mortal idioms." Merrick sighed. "I have been struggling with a lot, to be honest. What I feel for you is... it makes it difficult to think. My affections have also surpassed mere physical desires, and I care about you very much."

"What is there to think about?" Chase scooted a little closer. "I'm crazy about you. And you like me too. Can't we just... could we try?"

"I am worried about what will happen if I give in to my passions," Merrick replied softly. "We still have a job to do. We have sworn duties to uphold."

"And we can do it together," Chase promised. "Me and you."

"You make it sound so easy." Merrick smiled sadly.

"It can be," Chase said, his heart pounding so hard he was certain Merrick could hear it. "If you want me, I'm yours. That's kinda all there is to it."

"And if I do not?"

"Then I get over it." Chase's gut lurched. "I get over it, and we ain't gotta talk about this again. I've told you everything I wanted you to know."

"Just like that?" Merrick brought his other hand over to rest on top of Chase's. "You would not fight?"

"No."

"Why not?"

"It's like what Ollie was saying about his guy," Chase explained. "He could have tried to make Ted stay if he had told him the truth, but there wasn't any point if Ted didn't really love him. I wouldn't want you to be with me out of some fucked-up pity. I want you to want me because you just... want to."

"Oh, Elwood," Merrick murmured, "I very much want to.... It violates our code of conduct, the strict tenets against fraternization, and would bring into question whether or not we could be unbiased when evaluating each other's job performance."

Chase's heart squeezed in on itself deeper with every item that Merrick listed, and he really wanted another drink to soothe the pain. He knew there was always a chance Merrick would still reject him, but he had hoped....

"It's okay," Chase said suddenly, eager to go ahead and rip this Band-Aid off. "I get it. I know Merrick's career is your big priority." He pulled away. "I wanted you to know, and now you know, so—"

Merrick kissed him, hard, and didn't let go.

Hands fumbling, Chase wasn't sure if he should kiss back or not. He didn't understand what Merrick wanted him to do, and Chase had to stop him. "Wait, all that stuff, you just said—"

"Yes, all the reasons why this is a terrible idea."

"But then you kissed me!"

"I could have lost you twice today, and my most sincere regret would have been knowing I was letting mortal rules keep me from what I wanted," Merrick said firmly. "I still must insist we maintain the highest standards for our profession even though we are involving ourselves romantically. Merrick's career is very important to me, but… so are you."

"You mean that?" Chase asked as he searched Merrick's face, watching his eyes flicker from bright blue to those extraordinary black pools of stars. "We're really gonna do this?"

"If you still want me after how I wounded you," Merrick promised. "Yes."

"Nothin' but a scratch, baby boy," Chase gushed, and he leaned in for a deep kiss. "Mm, as long as you're not gonna suddenly change your fuckin' mind, okay? I'm all in now."

"I am also all in, as you say," Merrick said, his hands stroking Chase's beard. "I have never courted before, but I will do my best to ensure you feel loved and desired at all times."

"Off the clock, of course," Chase teased.

"Of course." Merrick bowed his head and kissed down Chase's neck, his tentacles unfurling from his sleeves. They reached out for Chase, hugged him close and worked at the buttons of his clothes.

"Before we get into any of that courting stuff," Chase panted, leaning into Merrick's hot mouth, "and that sounds really awesome, so very awesome, I gotta ask you somethin'."

"What is it, Elwood?"

"What exactly are the chances of me gettin' knocked up?"

CHAPTER 7.

MERRICK BURST out laughing, pulling back to grin up at Chase. "Bold of you to assume we are going to do anything that may potentially cause pregnancy."

"I did have my hopes." Chase chuckled, petting the side of Merrick's face. "Look, I'll do whatever you want, go as far as you're comfortable. But, uh, I am kinda curious about how this all works."

"Do you trust me?" Merrick asked with a warm smile.

"You know I do," Chase said.

"Then let me take care of you." Merrick leaned back in to kiss Chase and hold him close. "Mmm, I will show you pleasures your mortal mind has never known."

Chase wasn't about to argue with that, not with the seductive way Merrick's tentacles were peeling away his clothes as they kissed. A quick tentacle undid his tie and pulled away his jacket, and another removed his dress shirt, leaving him only in a thin white T-shirt. He was slowly being pushed down on the cushions, and Merrick's weight on top of him felt so good.

The sofa suddenly vanishing beneath him, not so good.

"What the fuck?" Chase jerked back to look around and find they were now in his bedroom, in the same position but now sprawled across his bed.

"You were not lying about the bedroom," Merrick remarked. "It is actually quite tolerable in here."

"Told you." Chase's heart fluttered to see Merrick smile at him like that, and he pulled him back in for another kiss. He could have kissed him like this for hours, never tiring of the sweet taste of his lips or all the wonderful little breathy sounds he made.

Chase's cock was throbbingly hard, and he couldn't remember the last time he had made out with someone like this. There wasn't any rush nor any real objective other than to kiss and feel good. Merrick was pressing close, petting Chase's hair and stroking the broad lines of his chest.

Chase reached out to slide Merrick's jacket off and let his hands move over Merrick's strong shoulders. He squeezed and ran his fingers back up over Merrick's hair. Merrick's tentacles were curling around him—his thighs, his hips, his arms—and it was wonderful. Weird, but fuck, if it wasn't amazing to know he was in the embrace of an immortal.

When one of the tentacles moved over Chase's hard cock, he jumped in surprise.

"Too fast?" Merrick asked breathlessly, and the tentacle curled back.

"No, you're okay, definitely okay," Chase panted. "Just weird when I feel your hands doing one thing, and I forget for a split second you got those other things. I'm good, I swear."

Merrick smiled and reached with his hands to unbutton Chase's pants. "Good. I am very eager to taste you. I have dreamed about it."

"Fuck," Chase whispered, filing that thought away for another conversation. He never had any clue that Merrick had these kinds of feelings for him. He touched Merrick's pants, palmed over his groin, but felt nothing. "Uh, you sure this is a dream come true?"

"Right." Merrick ducked his head sheepishly. "My human anatomy can function if you so choose."

"But would that feel good? I mean, tell me what to do." Chase set his jaw stubbornly. "Tell me how to make you feel good, Merr."

Merrick sat back, straddling Chase's hips as he removed his shirt and undershirt. His body was chiseled perfection, and Chase committed every taut line to memory as he took it all in. There were dark scars all around Merrick's arms, curling from around his shoulders and down to his wrists.

The scars lifted themselves right off his skin, turning a spectacular shade of green as they morphed into tentacles hidden in plain sight.

"The gods are all capable of miraculous means of reproduction," Merrick explained, "but the basic function is similar to yours. Some of our parts give pleasure, some receive it, and some do both."

Chase stared as a tentacle with a slit in the end caressed his chin. It looked like the same one he'd drank from earlier, and he touched it slowly. He saw Merrick shiver, and he stroked his fingers up and down the slick coil. "So, is this like giving you a hand job?"

"Yes," Merrick said, leaning forward and sliding his hands up Chase's round belly. "It is… it is very enjoyable."

"So, this one gives…?"

"It… it can do both." Merrick's eyes fluttered closed as Chase continued to stroke him. "I have… four… that can… mmm, *Elwood.*"

"Four that can do what?" Chase asked, bringing the tentacle to his lips to kiss it lightly. Judging by the way Merrick squirmed, the tentacle was particularly sensitive near the tip, and he focused a few soft kisses there.

"Give and receive, and I have two that only give," Merrick answered quickly, his hips rolling forward and grinding against Chase's hard cock. "Oh, Elwood. That, that feels very, very wonderful."

The pressure of Merrick's body on his dick was awesome, but Chase was determined to keep his attention on pleasuring Merrick if he could. He'd thought so long about having this man in his bed, and although it wasn't quite the way he'd pictured things—definitely more tentacles—he didn't want to waste a moment.

Merrick seemed to have ideas of his own, and his tentacles pushed Chase's arms down against the bed.

"What's wrong?" Chase asked urgently. "Was I not doin' it right?"

"You were doing an amazing job, but I meant it when I said I wanted to taste you. I have been very interested in exploring your body, and I am afraid I simply cannot wait." Merrick's tentacles slipped down into Chase's pants and pulled his cock out. "Oh! Wow…. *Elwood.*"

Chase allowed himself a very smug smile. He was definitely more than above average in that particular department, and the awestruck look on Merrick's face was pretty satisfying. "Yeah, well. Some guys got looks, some got brains, some of us got this."

"I happen to think you have all three in abundance," Merrick said as one of the thicker slitted tentacles came over to suck on the head of Chase's fat cock. "Although, I must confess, you have one of the most lovely specimens I have ever seen."

"Ah fuck," Chase gasped, watching the slit at the end of the tentacle open up like a mouth and swallow him down. No easy feat considering his size, and he was left panting as the tentacle took him all the way to the base of his dick. Nothing could compare to the magical pressure hugging his shaft, and the inside of the tentacle felt so hot and wet.

Gritting his teeth, Chase had to fight not to come instantly. The tentacle was sucking harder, pulsating in an unnatural and wonderful way, and there was a fantastic warmth washing over his whole body. There were goose bumps prickling his skin, sweat beading on his brow, and his nipples were getting hard.

"Ohh...." Merrick moaned softly, his mouth hanging open in a joyful smile. "Elwood, you... you are so big... I can feel you stretching me out...."

"I don't wanna hurt you," Chase managed to grunt. He was suddenly worried because he didn't know if a big dick could hurt a god. It sounded stupid in his head, but he still said, "You can slow down, baby boy. You ain't gotta take it all like that."

"I most certainly do," Merrick huffed as he leaned down to kiss him.

Chase groaned, kissing back eagerly as the tentacle continued to suck his cock. Being held down like this made him feel so small and vulnerable in spite of the difference in their physical size, and it gave him such an exciting thrill. This wasn't just any mortal man on top of him, but an actual god who was gobbling up every inch of his cock like he couldn't get enough.

It was nothing like anything he'd ever experienced before, and he knew he was going to bust at any second. He had wanted Merrick for so long, and this was more fantastic and intense than he could have ever imagined. "Mmm... Merr... I'm... I'm gonna—"

"Come on," Merrick panted against Chase's lips. "Please. I want to taste you, Elwood."

"Coming!" Chase groaned, his entire body tensing up before letting go in a blissful wave as his orgasm took over. He couldn't keep still, and his hips thrust up into the tentacle as it swallowed down his load. The pressure increased all around his cock as it took every drop, and Chase didn't know when it was going to end.

He was still coming in short jerks, and his arms flexed against the tentacles holding him in place. He couldn't believe it hadn't stopped yet. Tears were filling his eyes, and he panted frantically as the feeling teetered on the edge of pain from its intensity. His skin was tingling and aching, and every nerve was on fire from such a rush.

Merrick was watching him with the most adoring smile, stroking his hair and his chest as he soothed, "There... just like that. Just like that. Relax... you are doing so well."

The avalanche of sensation finally subsided, and Chase moaned loudly in both pleasure and relief. He went limp, struggling to catch his breath. "Wow."

"You taste even more lovely than I thought you would." Merrick bowed his head for a soft kiss. "Absolutely perfect."

As soon as Chase could move his arms, he wrapped them around Merrick and held him close. His heart was still beating so fast that he was worried it was going to pop, and he kissed Merrick in between gasps of breath.

"I would like to formally offer my intentions to court you, Elwood Q. Chase," Merrick said, bumping their noses together.

"Is that like dating for gods?" Chase asked with a short laugh.

"Yes, I suppose it is."

"Then yeah, I totally accept your courting," Chase replied. "I'll take anything you give me."

"You shall never be left wanting," Merrick assured him.

"I swear we'll make this work," Chase said. "With the job, I mean. I know that's important to you. For Merrick. The other Merrick. Shit." He cringed. "What am I supposed to call you?"

"Address me as you always have," Merrick replied. "Using 'Gordoth' may draw too much attention, and I like it when you call me 'Merry' in particular. It's not my true name, yes, but it's not Merrick's either. It feels like it's all mine, a special name that you gave me."

"Merry it is," Chase confirmed. He rubbed Merrick's back, stroking up to his shoulders. He could feel where the tentacles were rooted, idly tracing a finger around each one. There had to be at least a dozen. "These are pretty awesome, by the way. I would have been happy with some ordinary mortal penis, but these are nice."

Chuckling, Merrick kissed Chase's bearded cheek. "I am glad they please you."

"What about me pleasing them?" Chase licked his lips purposefully. "I mean, does one pop off and you're good? Or do all of them need some attention?"

Merrick shyly glanced away. "I do not need to experience orgasm with all of them to feel satisfied, but it is very pleasant."

"Well, come on, then," Chase said eagerly. "You've got what? Six all together for sexy times, right?"

"Yes, but you do not need to do that—"

"Well, I'd better go ahead and get started," Chase declared. "Come on, Merry. Let me."

"I am considering it." Merrick sat back on Chase's hips and slid his hands over Chase's stomach. Merrick then grabbed the hem of Chase's T-shirt and pushed it up.

"Hey," Chase protested, pulling his shirt back down.

"What is wrong?" Merrick stopped immediately, and he looked concerned.

"Just lemme keep it on, okay?" Chase said, and he grabbed the closest slitted tentacle he saw to redirect Merrick's attention.

"Are you not comfortable with your body?"

"Of fuckin' course not. Have you seen it?"

"Of what I can see, it is quite beautiful," Merrick replied without hesitation. "I think all of you is very pleasing."

"Thank you. You're insane, but thanks." Chase's face got hot, and he didn't want to linger on this. "For now, let's just, you know, keep some stuff on."

"For now," Merrick agreed.

Chase recognized that stubborn look in Merrick's eyes, and he knew his partner already had a new mission. He didn't want to give him another spare moment to plot, and he promptly stuck the tentacle he'd grabbed into his mouth.

"Ah!" Merrick gasped, his hands twisting in Chase's shirt.

Chase had meant to start off slow, but he was already cramming as much as he could down his throat and listening to Merrick moan and cry out. He swirled his tongue all around the tentacle and sucked hard, using his lips to maintain a steady pressure as he slid it in and out of his mouth.

He reached out for another tentacle, spying a thick one coiled up by his arm. He stroked it once he saw the telltale slit, squeezing and rubbing his finger over it. He watched as Merrick twitched, and then he felt Merrick's whole body shudder.

"Oh, Elwood." Merrick tipped his head back with a deep moan, tugging at Chase's shirt. "You are so very good at that. So very good! Please! More, give me more, do not stop!"

In the heat of the moment, Chase didn't think to grab a third tentacle for his other hand. Instead, he wrapped both hands around the one he'd been stroking and grunted as Merrick thrust the one in his mouth. He breathed in through his nose in quick bursts, relaxing his throat as the tentacle there went even deeper.

He could taste a hint of sweetness, and he knew Merrick had to be close. He moaned, the sound muffled but desperate, and he opened his mouth as wide as he could to let Merrick fuck his throat as hard as he wanted to.

"Oh, Elwood, oh, my darling, yes, yes, yes," Merrick chanted, his breathing hitting a nearly feverish rhythm. "Yes, yes, there, yes! Please! There!"

Chase felt the tentacle *swell* in his mouth when Merrick came, flooding his mouth and his throat until he was about to choke. He closed his eyes, focusing on swallowing as the tentacle's brutal pace slowed to a lazy crawl.

"That was wonderful," Merrick praised. "Oh, my darling. Your mouth is an absolute treasure. I cannot believe you—oh! Elwood!"

Chase had pulled the spent tentacle out of his mouth and shoved the one he'd been jerking off in. He slid his tongue around it in short little strokes, urging Merrick to thrust again.

"Elwood! Oh *fuck*!" Merrick was shaking again, and his head slumped against Chase's chest. "Yes, you can have them. You can have them all. Please! Please do not stop!"

Chase lifted his head up from the bed as he eagerly sucked the tentacle, and he grunted when he felt two new ones slide into his hands. He curled his fingers around them both and stroked quickly, matching the new pace Merrick set as he pushed back down Chase's throat.

He loved the slick, hot taste of the tentacle's flesh gliding over his lips, and the ones in his hands felt so thick and powerful. He teased the slits with the ends of his fingers before jerking them again, marveling at how they were already starting to leak.

Amazingly, he realized he was getting hard again, and there was a fresh wave of heat building up in his loins. It was his every fantasy come to life—the unbridled passion of sharing multiple partners at the same time and yet being able to capture the thrill of an all-out with one man, the man he loved.

No, his mind corrected, with the *god* he loved.

Merrick shouted Chase's name when he came again, and Chase swallowed down every delicious drop of his load. He barely had a second to breathe before the tentacle in his right hand was diving into his mouth to replace the one that had just spilled. He couldn't believe his jaw wasn't hurting yet, and he let Merrick have his way with him again.

The next load came faster, and Chase's thoughts were fogging over. There was an amazing sense of euphoria overtaking him, and he was lost to the sweet taste of Merrick's come. He felt younger, stronger, and completely revitalized.

By the time he'd taken the fourth load, he swore he was actually floating. His tongue and his lips were tingling, his skin was incredibly sensitive, and his cock was throbbing so hard it ached. He couldn't stop staring at Merrick, trying to memorize exactly what his face had looked like every time he'd climaxed.

Merrick kissed him, deep and slow, cradling Chase's face and petting his beard. "Elwood, you might be the most perfect being in all of Aeon. No one has ever made me feel such things."

"Mm, ain't done yet," Chase mumbled, sliding his tongue briefly into Merrick's mouth. "Two more still to go, right?"

"Oh, Elwood." Merrick groaned softly, and he kissed Chase again. "You are magnificent. If you truly want them, they are yours."

Chase grinned. "Bring it on, baby boy. I'm ready. I can take anything you got."

When Merrick actually presented his final set of tentacles, Chase briefly regretted that last statement.

The tentacles were big.

No, they were *huge*.

They were far more phallic than the others, with pointed, defined heads and small ridges running around the shafts. They also had bulbous knots about a foot down from the tip. One was only slightly smaller than the other in terms of girth, but they both made Chase's own sizable cock look rather diminutive by comparison.

It was gonna be like trying to cram a damn soda can in his mouth.

"Holy fuck," Chase whispered, staring stupidly at the pair of tentacle-cocks.

"If you are not comfortable with proceeding, I would completely understand," Merrick swore. "These are made only for giving pleasure, you see, for mating."

"The getting pregnant kinda mating?"

"Yes, but accidentally spawning is impossible," Merrick soothed. "There must be intent for it to happen. I cannot get you pregnant unless I wanted to, no more than I could spawn a child without my own innate desire."

"Putting a pin in that for now, good to know." Chase tentatively reached for the smaller of the tentacle-cocks. He licked the pointed tip, gathering up spit to wet his lips so he could start sucking.

Merrick rolled off Chase and over onto his side, urging Chase to turn toward him with a few tugs of his tentacles. He ran his fingers through Chase's hair, pulling lightly as he sighed contentedly. He didn't move the tentacle in Chase's mouth but instead let him take it at his own pace.

Chase tried stroking the length of the tentacle-cock that he couldn't fit in his mouth—which was pretty much all of it except the head and the first few inches—and focused his tongue on the ridges around the tip.

He could feel more tentacles moving over his body, and his pants and underwear were being pulled down to his knees. His mind was racing with what Merrick might be up to, and he moaned when he felt the second tentacle-cock slip between his thighs.

"Is this all right?" Merrick asked, giving an experimental thrust. "May I take my pleasure like this?"

"Mmph." Chase closed his legs together tightly, and he shivered at the way the tentacle-cock rubbed up against his balls and the base of his dick. He pulled off long enough to reply, "Yeah, that. Come on. It feels fuckin' good."

"Yes, mm, yes, it does," Merrick replied, smiling wide as he thrust between Chase's thighs. He was pushing at just the right angle for the head of his tentacle-cock to tease against Chase's hole, and some of the previously spent tentacles moved to attend to Chase's hard cock.

Once again blown away by so much simultaneous stimulation, Chase found himself whimpering and struggling to keep up. He could barely maintain any friction on the tentacle-cock in his mouth because of the way he was moaning, grinding down on the one between his legs as the other tentacles sucked and squeezed his dick and balls.

He was suddenly consumed by thoughts of actually taking one of those monstrous tentacles *inside* of him, thinking about how stretched out and open he would be, and he came even harder than before.

There was a flood of heat as Merrick came between Chase's legs mere moments after, leaving Chase's thighs dripping as his orgasm continued to shake him from head to toe. He sobbed in pleasure, caught up in the incredible suction around his cock and the sudden splash of more come in his mouth as Merrick came again, his own blissful moans joining Chase's.

Chase swallowed and suckled down all he could, but he was so dizzy that he thought he might pass out. He threw his arms around Merrick and smothered his face into his chest, trembling erratically. "Oh fuck... oh my gods... Merr... mmm... fuck!"

Merrick held him tightly and rubbed his back, pressing sweet kisses all through his hair. "Yes, my darling. Yes... just let it take you.... You are almost there."

On the verge of tears, Chase inhaled shakily and breathed his way through the intense waves of pleasure. They dwindled away as Merrick withdrew his many tentacles, and Chase was exhausted. His body felt heavy, warm, and he never wanted to leave this bed ever again.

"You were amazing," Merrick gushed as he cuddled up close. "I am very pleased that we are courting, Elwood. I am so happy that... that you are mine."

"Yours," Chase agreed. "Mmph, what time is it?"

"Almost eight o'clock," Merrick replied. "We have been, well, quite busy."

"I don't even know where my phone is." Chase laughed. "Fuck. This has been... wow, it's been amazing."

"Wait here." Merrick kissed him. "I will retrieve it. It would be irresponsible of us not to keep in touch with the department."

"Sure thing." Chase smiled. He fully enjoyed the view of Merrick's naked butt as he walked back out into the living room, and once Chase had his pants pulled back up, he flopped against the bed with a satisfied groan.

Wow.

That was the only thought constantly repeating through his mind, and he was still smiling like a complete fool when Merrick came back with his phone.

"Thanks," he said, flipping through the notifications to read some new texts.

"Anything important?" Merrick asked as he slid back into bed beside him.

"Ollie is almost done translating the first painting," Chase said, wagging his eyebrows. "Wanna hear the latest exploits of Lord Collins and his meaty shaft?"

"Is it in any possible way going to be helpful or related to the case?"

"Might be. Maybe. Dunno." Chase shrugged. "Won't know unless we read it."

Merrick grimaced. "Carry on, then, if you feel that you must."

"Ah, so, Lord Collins has just given his meaty shaft over to the maid, and her willing moist channels have happily received him...."

"How much more is there?"

"Lots."

CHAPTER 8.

ALTHOUGH READING the raunchy erotica was wildly entertaining, it was not useful for their case. Ollie had begun translating the second painting, and those findings were only slightly more helpful.

"Make your holy pledge to Salgumel where the veil is most weak," Chase read out loud. "You must say all his sacred words to find what you seek. To enter his dreams, cross land at the seams, where the rivers run dry, the birds fly, and... men don't speak?"

Merrick frowned.

"What the fuck does that mean?"

"The veils between the worlds of Aeon, Xenon, and Zebulon are weak here in Archersville," Merrick offered. "It is a prime location for rituals of this kind."

"And the rest of it?"

"I do not know."

"Why can't they ever just say 'go here by this damn tree'?" Chase huffed. "Or 'light this candle by this giant rock with this conveniently placed sign'?"

"It would not be as mystical, I suppose." Merrick snorted. "The harder it is to explain, the more mystical something is."

"Mystical, huh?" Chase glanced over at Merrick, eyeing the full length of his body. "I'd say what we just did is pretty damn mystical, because I can't even begin to explain what you did to me."

"Would you like me to tell you? Perhaps in the same style as the ever-vivid Lord Collins?" Merrick smiled, reaching out to caress Chase's cheeks. "Mm, I suppose you might enjoy that a little too much."

"Probably." Chase caught Merrick's hand and kissed each one of his fingers and his palm. "Might get me all riled up again."

"It does not take much, does it?" Merrick chuckled fondly.

"With you? Nah." Chase stretched his legs with a little grunt. "I'll need to freshen up before we go again, though. Maybe a light snack. Like some—"

He hadn't even finished speaking before they were both naked, clean, and tucked under the covers. There was also a silver platter of donuts at the foot of the bed and a six-pack of beer.

"Wow."

"Is this satisfactory?" Merrick asked, daring to look concerned.

"Fuck, you're amazing." Chase pulled the sheets high up on his chest as he sat up to snag a beer. Even after what they'd just done, he felt a little awkward about showing certain parts of his body. He popped the beer open and took a swig, delighted to find it was ice-cold. He lay back down with a very pleased sigh.

"Mmm, that is a good look on you." Merrick reached over to run his fingers through Chase's hair.

"Huh?" Chase slurped noisily at his beer. "What's that?"

"Happy." Merrick's smile could have lit up the entire city.

"Yeah?" Chase was certain his own smile was equally luminous as he grinned at Merrick. "Stick around, and I guarantee you'll see more of it."

"I plan to," Merrick assured him.

After taking another drink of his beer, Chase asked, "And you really had a thing for me all of this time?"

"Now who's the inadequate detective?" Merrick smirked, and one of his tentacles curled around Chase's arm. "You really do not give yourself enough credit. I found you very fascinating, and I must admit I became quite infatuated with you fairly quickly."

Merrick shivered as another tentacle draped itself over his belly beneath the sheets. "Ditto, baby boy." He chugged the rest of his beer, burped, and tossed the empty can on the floor. "Excuse me. I swear I'll pick it up later."

"Ah, it is a wonder how I was ever able to resist you," Merrick drawled.

"Hey, I am very charming," Chase argued, grabbing Merrick and pulling him up on his chest. "Not to mention hilarious."

Merrick snuggled in close, resting his head on Chase's shoulder. He traced the freckles dotting his collarbone. "I suppose that is what first got my attention. You always knew how to make me laugh." He paused. "That and your voluptuous behind."

"My *what*?"

"You heard me."

"So the god of justice likes his men curvy?"

"Perhaps." Merrick continued to draw little lines between Chase's freckles, moving down to his chest right above the edge of the sheet. "My sense of attraction is not dependent upon a set of specific variables. I find many things pleasing."

"Glad old gingers with voluptuous behinds made the cut."

"I have spent much of my life waiting for a perfect mate," Merrick said quietly. "There was a time when I did have an ideal candidate in mind, and I wasted centuries trying to find someone that met my impossible standards without success."

"The love goddess." Chase recalled the prediction Merrick had received. "That's what she meant about not waiting around for perfect?"

"Yes, because my perfect mate was already right in front of me." Merrick leaned up for a tender kiss, several more tentacles curling around Chase's body and holding him close.

The kiss lingered, deep and slow, and Chase slipped his tongue into Merrick's mouth to explore and taste. The earlier urgency had been well sated, but it wouldn't have taken much for Chase to get going again.

A yawn interrupted his lusty ambitions, and he had to turn his head to cover his mouth. "Sorry. Shit, it's not even that late. Your perfect mate might need a nap."

"It is all right," Merrick soothed. "I do not mind waiting a little longer. Besides, we have to get up early to arrange transport to the precinct. After the morning briefing, our first order of business will be visiting Mr. Romero."

"Sir, yes, sir," Chase said obediently, getting settled down for sleep. He was so relaxed that it wouldn't take long for him to doze off. "Good night, Merry."

"Good night, my darling," Merrick replied. "Sleep well."

Even as Chase's mind drifted, there was something Merrick had said that stuck out as a bit strange. "Hey, Merry."

"Yes?"

"What did you mean by waiting a little longer? A little longer for what?"

"To mate." Merrick's tentacles hugged Chase. "To have sex."

"A lot of couples do," Chase mumbled, ignoring the stirring in his loins as he started thinking about what mating with Merrick would be like. "It's not a big deal. Ain't gotta rush anything."

"As I said, I do not mind waiting," Merrick said. "I want my first time to be special."

"Whatever you want, baby." Chase was almost asleep before his eyes popped back open. "Wait? Your first time?" He squinted at Merrick. "Are you… are you a virgin?"

"Of course I am," Merrick scoffed, lifting his head to frown at Chase. "They call me Gordoth the Untouched. What did you think it meant?"

"I don't know!" Chase sputtered. He was stunned, to say the least. "Wait, so, all the tentacle orgies? You didn't do any of that stuff?"

"No." Merrick frowned. "I would share my seed in ritual bowls as offerings if our worshippers desired to imbibe it, but I never shared it as I have with you." He fidgeted. "Does this displease you?"

"Not at all," Chase said quickly. "I'm just, well, a little surprised is all. I'm honored. Flattered. Both. That you wanna do that with me. I mean, really. All of these gazillions of years and you didn't want to?"

"I very much wanted to, but my desires were to wait until I found the perfect mate." Merrick laid his head back down. "The longer I waited, the more impossible it seemed. It felt wrong to simply give myself away for the sake of doing it when I had withheld on principle for so long. Once we were all in the dreaming, I began to accept that I wouldn't ever share it with someone."

"Well, you got me now," Chase said softly, his heart clenching up. "And I dunno about perfect, but well—" He grinned. "—I'm pretty damn close."

"Your humility is admirable." Merrick chuckled.

"I do kinda wish I had known. I coulda tried to be better. Not that I wasn't good, because I'm always good, but you know… just would have taken my time, I mean."

"I am sorry I made such assumptions. I know how ignorant you are."

"Wow." Chase snorted. "Be still my heart."

"Elwood, I meant no offense!" Merrick sighed in frustration. "I am terrible at this."

"It's okay." Chase guided Merrick back in for a reassuring kiss. "Totally okay. We'll go as fast or as slow as you want to. I love you, Merry. I really fuckin' do. I'll do whatever you want, okay? All I wanna do is make you happy."

"I love you too," Merrick whispered in reply, seemingly in awe he was saying those words out loud. "I am... I am very pleased to hear that. There is truly no one else I could ever want to be my first."

"Good. I fuckin' swear I'll make it so good for you, baby." Chase fought to stifle another yawn. "We can plan the whole thing out. I'll get you flowers, some candles, whatever you want."

"Perhaps we should discuss all of this tomorrow," Merrick said with a light chuckle. "Once we are off duty, of course."

"Of course." Chase kissed him again before getting ready for sleep once more. The lights magically turned off, and the rest of the beer and neglected donuts vanished. Seeing such a casual display of power added to Chase's rising nerves.

Courting a god was already an intimidating task, but now knowing he was going to be the one to take his virginity?

Yeah, no pressure.

Not to mention they still had a gang of cultists out there trying to summon some other god who would destroy the world when he woke up.

No pressure at all.

In spite of his anxious thoughts about bedding a god and trying to stop another from annihilating humanity, Chase slept better than he had in years. He woke up before his alarm even went off and found himself cradled in a warm nest of tentacles.

He'd rolled over on his side during the night and was holding Merrick against his chest, and Merrick's tentacles were wrapped around them both. He didn't move right away, taking a few moments to admire his partner's sleeping face.

"Good morning," Merrick said, opening his eyes and smiling at him.

Okay, not sleeping.

"Morning." Chase smirked. "I guess you don't actually need to sleep, do you?"

"No more than I need to eat. I do enjoy it, though. The eating, I mean. The sleeping is also nice to rest my mind. It has become a bit of a habit."

"Mmm." Chase kissed him and got such a warm thrill from the very fact he could do that whenever he wanted now. "Well, if you like eating, I'll have to cook for you. Always wanted to."

"You cook?" Merrick was unable to hide his surprise.

"Yeah, I know my kitchen looks like something died in there, but I swear I can."

"All of the takeout delivery men know you by name."

"Okay, so it's been a little while." Chase laughed. "I didn't see a point in cooking for just me."

"I would like that very much," Merrick said, leaning in for another kiss. His tentacles pulled Chase flush against him, and he slid his hands over Chase's shoulders.

Right as Chase slipped Merrick his tongue to deepen their kiss, he heard his phone ringing. "Shit. Phone." He grumbled as he pulled away to find it and grumbled more when he saw it was dispatch calling. He sat up, putting the call on speaker. "Yo. Detective Chase here."

"Hey, Chase!" It was Milo, sounding far too cheerful to be up this early.

"Milo?" Chase frowned. "What the hell are you doing calling from dispatch?"

"Oh, I came in to work early 'cause my girlfriend sent me out at, like, two o'clock for green tea ice cream and chicken nuggets. Couldn't go back to sleep and, well, apparently nobody else wanted to call you 'cause they figured you'd be *busy* with Detective Merrick."

"Busy?"

"I mean, he's still over at your place, right?" Milo sounded like he was grinning, that cheeky little bastard. "Both of your cars are still here."

Refusing to answer any of that, Chase grunted in annoyance. The last thing they needed was the rumor mill starting up. "What's up, Milo?"

"Slappy Romero. He's dead."

"What the fucking fuck?"

"Maid called it in when she came in to clean the house," Milo replied. "A couple of uniforms are already there, secured the scene, but you should probably get moving."

"You're our forensics guy!" Chase huffed. "Why aren't you over there?"

"Uh, duh, my shift doesn't start until eight."

Chase bit the side of his phone.

"Mr. Evans," Merrick coolly interjected, "you do realize performing any departmental duties without being clocked in is a direct violation of both state law and our precinct policies. I am very confident you did not ask for any supervisor approval regarding this unexpected overtime, so if you want our support to ensure you get paid, I am sure you would not mind heading to the scene a little earlier for us."

"Yes, sir," Milo squeaked.

"Goodbye, Mr. Evans." Merrick smirked as he pushed the button to end the call.

"Well, shit." Chase grinned. "Look at you. Savage takedown."

"Any abuse of the system will not be tolerated on my watch," Merrick declared with his head held high. He sunk back down as he added, "Although by speaking up, I did confirm his suspicions about my location."

"How about you forget about all that and abuse my mouth with some of those tentacle-dicks?" Chase purred, snatching one he found familiar and mouthing his way down toward the tip.

"We need to get ready for work," Merrick scolded even as his eyes fluttered.

"I can be so very quick." Chase licked the tip of the tentacle. "Quick like a bunny."

"Mmm, you had better be."

Chase was able to get Merrick to come at least three times and earn himself a spectacular orgasm before Merrick finally dragged him out of bed. They took turns showering, got dressed, and grabbed a cab to take them over to the precinct.

The sun was up, the birds were all chirping, and Chase couldn't stop smiling. Even though they were going to be headed over to a crime scene, he was in a very good mood. He didn't even care that the coffee from the precinct's break room was nearly as burned as his hat. He had just spent the night with the man he loved, and he had never been so happy.

They informed dispatch of where they were going and went back outside to get Merrick's car. The temptation to reach over and grab Merrick's hand was strong, but Chase resisted.

They were on duty now, and they had to behave.

Specifically, Chase had to behave.

Other than a little smile as they got out of the car at Mr. Romero's house, Merrick had given no indication than anything between them had changed. The dispatchers had definitely been eyeballing the two of them earlier, perhaps hoping for some sort of tell, but Merrick hadn't given them a thing.

Chase wasn't sure if he had, but it was impossible to hide how happy he was. His cheeks were sore from smiling so much, and he was worried he was being obvious.

As they entered the lush three-story home, he did his best to put on a serious face and not think about how sweet Merrick's lips had tasted, or how soft his skin was, or all those amazing things those tentacles could do....

Damn.

"Good morning!" Milo greeted them as they walked into the marble-floored foyer. "Detective Chase, very special Detective Merrick. Welcome to Slappy Romero's humble home."

Merrick rolled his eyes and sighed.

"Nothing humble about these digs," Chase remarked, glancing over the fancy surroundings. "Pretty sure that damn chair over there is worth more than my car."

"Probably." Milo headed upstairs, waving for them to follow. "Come on, dudes. I'll show you what we got. You're gonna love it."

"Somehow I doubt that," Merrick said dryly.

"Unless you happen to have video footage of the murder and a taped confession," Chase chimed in.

"Almost as good," Milo said mysteriously, ushering them into a lush office.

It had all the usual things that most offices did—a desk, a chair, some stacks of files, a few letters, and a modest computer setup.

It also had a corpse.

There was a dead man with a thick beard in a bathrobe on the floor in front of the desk, and his heart had been removed as before. The walls were covered with expensive-looking paintings, but there was a curious blank spot above the desk.

"So, that down there is Mr. Slappy," Milo said, pausing as he turned to point up at the empty spot on the wall. "And that up there was our genuine Lord Collins painting."

"Stolen," Chase griped.

"Ah! But wait!" Milo bounced over to the desk and began typing on the computer. He clicked something and turned the monitor toward Chase and Merrick with a proud smile.

A video was playing, footage from a security camera aimed right at the front door. A man in a big coat walked into the frame, and Chase recognized him as Jeffrey Martin.

"Holy shit," Chase scoffed as he watched Jeffrey letting himself into the house. "I'll fuckin' be."

Milo clicked again, fast forwarding until Jeffrey was seen walking back out with the painting. "Boom! Okay, so we got Jeff coming in and going out with his precious painting. No murder weapon, but his prints are all over the front door."

"How did he get in?"

"He had a key."

"Why didn't he just portal in?" Chase wondered out loud. "Wards?"

"Many," Merrick confirmed. "I saw them when we came inside. Mr. Romero was very concerned about his safety. He was using very powerful magic that would prevent any mortal teleportation."

"Not concerned enough," Chase quipped. "He let somebody have a fuckin' key to his house, and then Jeffy came on in and killed the crap out of him." He scratched his head. "Any connection between Jeff and Slappy?"

"None that I've been able to find," Milo replied. "I'm going to keep looking through his records, but so far we've got nothing. They both went to the same prison, but not at the same time. Slappy was there first, and he got out before Jeff got sent up."

Chase idly poked at the letters on top of the desk, noting there was no return address. Instead, there was a little doodle of a flower. It looked so familiar....

"We can still totally slap some more murder charges on Jeffy boy when you guys find him," Milo continued on excitedly. "We have the prints, the security footage, and I'm sure we'll find his DNA on Slappy's body."

"But how did Mr. Martin know to come here?" Merrick challenged. "If they have no known social connections, as you say, it is very strange that he had a key."

"Maybe some kinda enchanted skeleton key?"

"No residue on the door," Merrick said, because of course he knew that. "The painting was last reported stolen from Mr. Romero's gallery, and his home address is unlisted."

"Tracking glyph," Milo suggested. "Watchman spell. There's a bunch of different ways to find someone. Maybe he followed Slappy here from the gallery once they figured out that the stolen one was a fake?"

"No, there is no trace of a spell having been cast on Mr. Romero." Merrick scowled.

"Well, fine! Then you come up with something!" Milo hissed, throwing up his hands. "I'm not the detective here! Can't you, ahem, *divine* something?"

"Even I have to work with evidence. It would be helpful if you could provide some."

Chase continued to walk the perimeter of the room to look around, and he found a framed photograph of Mr. Romero. It was him posing in front of the Lord Collins painting in this very room, but he didn't have his big beard. It must have been several years ago.

Merrick and Milo continued to argue, and Chase headed back over to the desk. He saw the letters again and picked one up. When he looked at the flower, he remembered where he'd seen it before. "Hey."

"What is it, Detective Chase?" Merrick asked.

"Look," he said, holding out the letter. "I saw this same stupid flower on some letters over at Martin's house."

"Oh, right," Milo said. "Mr. Martin was part of a prison pen pal thing when he was in. People write letters to inmates and stuff. Daisy was supposed to find out who it was."

"Looks like these are from when our pal Slappy was in." Chase pointed to the prison address and the date. "We need to find out who was writing to both of these guys, like, yesterday."

"I'll call Daisy right now," Milo promised, reaching for his phone.

Chase felt a strange lurch in his stomach. The flower—

"Would reading the letters be too obvious of a suggestion?" Merrick interrupted his thought process.

"Huh? Eat me." Chase peeked inside the envelope and made a face. The writing within looked like total gibberish. He showed it to Merrick. "Any idea what that shit says?"

"No."

"More godstongue?"

"No. It is some kind of cipher." Merrick glanced over to Milo chatting away on the phone. He lowered his voice, saying, "Perhaps we could use your nephew's starsight."

"Wait, who has starsight?" Milo asked, still on the phone but staring at them curiously.

Chase grimaced and snapped, "Mind your damn beeswax, Milo!"

"Sheeeesh, sorry." Milo pouted and returned to his conversation with Daisy. "He's so grumpy. Maybe you-know-what didn't actually go down with you-know-who."

"We can hear you." Merrick narrowed his eyes and *growled*. "Gossip will not be tolerated—"

"Come over here, grumpy." Chase grabbed Merrick's shoulder and gently steered him away. "Okay, listen. Martin is still in the wind, but maybe we can get Ollie to look over these letters. I can have Milo send us the ones from the other crime scene too. Maybe even try that photo of Slappy posing with the legit painting?"

"Milo can totally do that!" Milo called out.

"Stop eavesdropping, nosy ass!" Chase barked. "Find out who the hell sent those letters!" He sighed in frustration and turned back to Merrick.

"Well, now what?" Merrick asked.

"First, we get breakfast because I'm fuckin' starving," Chase replied. "Then we'll go see Ollie and pray he's sober enough to read this stuff."

CHAPTER 9.

THE DRIVE over to Ollie's house was quiet except for Chase's munching. After leaving Mr. Martin's house, they had stopped at a fast-food restaurant for some greasy breakfast. Merrick had declined, but Chase ordered two different value meals.

"You sure you don't want something?" Chase offered a deep-fried hash brown.

"I'm very sure." Merrick gave Chase a small smile before quickly looking back to the road.

Chase finished eating, tucked the trash inside the bag, and wiped his hands off on his pants. He paused, choosing to use the neglected napkins at the bottom of the bag instead before balling everything up.

He could do with being a little cleaner. He was dating a god now, after all.

"What kind of stuff do you like to eat?" Chase asked suddenly. "Like, what's your favorite thing?"

"Favorite?"

"I wanna know what to make you for dinner," Chase explained. "I know you have a heck of a sweet tooth, but what about savory stuff? Steak? Pasta?"

"My tooth is not sweet."

"You don't drink coffee unless it's obliterated with sugar and creamer, and you always eat cake icing first."

Merrick pouted indignantly.

"So?" Chase prompted.

"I will be pleased by whatever you want to make me," Merrick said shortly. "Now, we should focus on the case. At this time, we must assume the cultists have all of the available paintings."

Chase tried to ignore how much Merrick's brisk attitude stung, but it still hurt. "You know there's no one listening in right now, yeah?"

"We are still on duty," Merrick reminded him. "It would not be appropriate to discuss anything that involves our personal relationship."

"Yeah, right. I got it." Chase did his best not to be upset, and he turned his attention to watching the buildings pass by as they continued to drive. He frowned when Merrick took a right when he should have made a left. "Wait, what are you doing?"

Merrick didn't say anything, making another right into a parking garage.

"Did I fuck up?" Chase asked with a nervous laugh. "Uh, seriously, did I piss you off or something?"

"No," Merrick replied curtly as he parked in an isolated corner. "Take your coat off and put it over your lap."

"What?"

"You heard me." Merrick's eyes were dark when he looked at Chase. "You require some kind of reassurance, yes? You are obviously not happy with me."

"Hey!" Chase gasped when Merrick's tentacles slipped out from his jacket sleeves and went right for his pants. "It's not a big deal! I just wanted to talk about dinner is all! It doesn't mean you gotta do all this!"

"Physical affection is a very powerful way to express our devotion to each other," Merrick said, his tentacles pulling at Chase's zipper. "We will have to be quick because we are on duty, but I wish to ease your worries."

"Words! Talking! Also good ways to express devotion!" Chase managed to pull Merrick's stubborn tentacles away. "Listen, you don't have to suddenly put out just because I got a little upset!"

"No?"

"No!" Chase said earnestly. "Look, you wanted to keep work time professional, and I'm the one who was being pushy about dinner. If I gotta wait to clock out for you to tell me what you wanna eat, well, then that's what I gotta do."

"You will not be angry with me?" Merrick's tentacle squeezed Chase's hand.

"Because you set some boundaries that I plowed right through?" Chase shook his head. "No. I'll be fine. I'm a big boy, Merr. Yeah, it's gonna bug me because I don't wanna have to wait to talk to you about that kinda stuff, but what you want matters too."

"I want to make you happy," Merrick said, his jaw tightening. "I do not want you to think that I don't care about your needs. You are very important to me."

"And you're important to me," Chase soothed. "Right now, what's important is doing our jobs and getting over to Ollie's to see if he can help us catch some bad guys."

"You are truly not upset I didn't wish to discuss dinner plans?"

"I'm totally fine," Chase promised. "We can talk about it after work." He nudged Merrick's leg, teasing, "If you really feel that bad about it, I'm sure we can think up some ways for you to make it up to me later."

"Later? So you do not desire sex right now?"

"Nope." Chase could feel his face getting hot, and he willed his body to behave. "I'm good."

"I do not believe you."

"Yeah, well, you can not-believe me the whole way over to Ollie's. World to save, all that. We can figure out what I'm gonna feed you after we clock out for the day."

"I am looking forward to it," Merrick said as he backed up and exited the parking garage. "I have heard very promising things about frozen breadsticks."

"Not gonna lie, they're pretty damn good."

They arrived at Ollie's apartment without any other unexpected detours, and Chase knocked on the door.

Nothing.

Chase knocked again, waiting a few moments before knocking some more. There was still no answer, and he shouted, "Hey, Ollie! It's me! Open up, kiddo!"

Merrick glanced at his watch. "It's almost ten o'clock. Should he not be awake by now?"

"If he's drinking as hard as I think he is, he might still be passed the hell out," Chase muttered, banging his fist against the door.

"For fuck's sake!" Ollie's voice groaned from inside. The locks clicked and the door opened, revealing Ollie in nothing but a pair of shorts. His face was red and blotchy, and he looked like hell. "Uncle Elwood, what? It's so early. Like, way too early."

"Need your help again." Chase held up the letters. "Can you work that starsight voodoo on these for us?"

"Fine." Ollie rubbed at his eyes. "Just leave 'em here."

"I am afraid we must insist on expediting the translation," Merrick said. "Although your work on the paintings was very much appreciated, it did not give us enough information to find our suspect."

"Well, that sucks." Ollie yawned.

"Come on, Ollie," Chase urged. "This is serious."

"More world-saving type shit?" Ollie's shoulders sagged. "Fine." He waved them inside, holding out his hand for the letters. "What are these?"

"From a homicide victim's house," Chase explained. "He and our suspect were both in prison, and the same person was writing them. We're really hoping there's something useful in there."

Ollie shut the door behind them, and he flipped through the letters. "Where's the rest? These are all addressed to someone named 'Slappy.'"

Chase noticed there were new empty bottles of alcohol by the trash, and a half-empty one was beside the couch with a cluster of used tissues. There was a small photo album on the coffee table, but it was closed.

"We are waiting for forensics to deliver copies of them electronically to us," Merrick replied. "Can you please read those for now? This man has already killed once, and we suspect his involvement in another death."

"Kinda weird. A murderer named Slappy."

"Slappy is the victim," Chase corrected. He glanced over at the mess by the couch and casually asked, "You doing okay, kiddo?"

"I'm super." Ollie plopped down in the wicker chair. He pulled out the first letter. "Okay, blah blah blah, I miss you, it sucks you're in prison, can't wait to see you…." He paused. "And all hail our Lord Salgumel. It will be glorious when he is finally risen."

"And we have a winner," Chase declared. "Slappy and Martin were both in on the cult!"

"But if that is true, why did Slappy withhold the real painting?" Merrick pointed out. "Logically, he would have given it willingly if his goals were aligned with our cultists."

"Okay, so maybe he had a change of heart when he got out of prison," Chase suggested, taking a seat on the sofa. "Once he was a free man, he decided that he wasn't down with helping them wake up ol' Sally boy."

"And the mysterious pen pal recruited him to the cause using their womanly or manly wiles? What about them?"

"Womanly," Ollie piped up. "Based on the, uh, more neurotic sections of these letters, I would definitely say our writer is a lady."

"Do you mean 'erotic'?" Chase asked kindly.

"Yeah, that too."

Chase's phone beeped, and he glanced down to see Milo had sent him a bunch of photos. "Just got the rest of our letters. Milo got 'em all scanned in. Can I text them to you, Ollie?"

"Yeah," Ollie replied, grunting as he got up. "I've just gotta get my phone. Left it charging in my room."

"No problem." Chase began to forward the images, waiting until Ollie was away in his bedroom before he opened the photo album on the coffee table.

The first page was two men kissing, and Chase recognized them as Ollie and that giant guy, Ted, that he used to date. He flipped through a few more pages, and he grimaced when he realized it was an old album of their relationship together.

"What are you doing?" Merrick asked suspiciously.

"Detecting." Chase paused when he found a folded-up piece of paper. There were several statements written out, strange things like "Ted is dead," "Ted moved away," "Ted is still in love with me."

They were all crossed out except the very last one, and it read, "Ted is getting married."

"Hey!" Ollie suddenly shouted as he came back out. He stormed over and snatched up the album, scowling. "That's private shit, you jerk!"

"I'm sorry!" Chase held up his hands. "I was just lookin'."

Ollie sniffed defiantly, cradling the photo album against his chest. "Look, I know it's, like, super lame, but I'm working on it, okay? Moving on. I'm… I'm trying. I found out he's getting married, and he's all super happy… and I'm trying to get over it."

"The paper," Merrick said quietly. "You wrote out sentences and were able to recognize them as false or true because of your starsight?"

"Yeah." Ollie frowned. "I mean, sometimes. Uh. Sometimes what's hidden is a lie, and I can see it. But it kinda only works when… well, when I'm upset. And, like, really hammered."

"Could you just write down where these cultists are and, like, find them through process of elimination?" Chase suggested hopefully.

"Well, I'm not very upset at them right now, so no."

"Ending the world isn't upsetting enough?"

Ollie stalked back to his bedroom without a word with the photo album.

"It makes sense," Merrick said as he sat beside Chase. "The power of magic can often be fueled by emotion. For Oleander to attempt this kind of divination without formal training, he has to use his most raw feelings to power the spell."

"So he can only use his starsight to check up on his ex that he's very clearly still hot for?"

"It is a complicated gift," Merrick scolded. "To see all that is hidden has limitless possibilities, and Ollie has not had anyone helping him seek his full potential."

"First of all," Ollie said as he walked back in, "I can totally hear both of you talking about me. *Rude*. Thin walls in here. So thin. And uh, I got something after looking through Je-fahfah's letters, but you're probably not gonna like it."

"What is it?" Chase asked.

"It's this poem about talking to Salgumel that the flower girl wrote to Slappy. It's also in the letters you texted me that she sent to Je-fahfah, and in one of the paintings."

"Wait, why are you saying his name like that?"

"Like what?"

"Je-*fahfah*."

"There's two f's. Obviously."

"What did you find, Oleander?" Merrick asked politely, nudging Chase's leg to keep him quiet.

"To enter his dreams, you must cross land at the seams, where the rivers run dry, the souls fly, and men don't speak," Ollie recited. "They're talking about killing someone. A human sacrifice."

"The land at the seams! It must be referring to the veil between Aeon, Xenon, and Zebulon!" Merrick exclaimed, his eyes wide. "And the rivers run dry—"

"Xenon might have a bridge, but there's no water under it." Ollie looked quite proud of himself. "Souls flying are the souls flying through the bridge, and men ain't speakin'." He paused, then added, "You know, 'cause they're dead."

"Got it." Chase tried to think. "Well, that explains why Jeff has been chopping people up. This ritual needs some human flesh mojo to get going."

"There must be something wrong," Merrick said. "They must have some part of the ritual wrong, or perhaps the specifics of the sacrifice itself are not correct."

"That really doesn't make me feel better. We dunno how many paintings they have and how many of 'em were porn or what." Chase took off his hat to smooth his hands through his hair.

"I could... I could try to find out." Ollie returned to his wicker chair. "If you wanted me to try."

"How?"

"Text me something, like the bad guys have five paintings. And then the bad guys have seven of them. A whole list like that." Ollie grabbed the bottle by the sofa and turned it up. "Shit. Mm, okay. Come on, do it."

"And what, you'll be able to pick out which one is the lie?" Chase didn't understand. "But I wouldn't be lying because I honestly don't know how many they have!"

"No more than I knew about whether or not Ted was getting hitched," Ollie pointed out. "If I see it, fuckin' great. If not, I'll go back to reading more prison smut. Okay?"

"It's worth a try." Merrick shrugged. "Go on."

"Fine." Chase typed out a full text of the bad guys having X number of paintings from one to eight and sent them over.

Turning the bottle up again, Ollie chugged a few more gulps before turning his attention to his phone. "Okay. Here we go." He narrowed his eyes as he read, pausing before he said, "Okay, more than four but less than eight."

"That's… marginally helpful." Chase grimaced.

"Look, I can tell they have more than four, but them having five is a lie. Like they lost one or something. They definitely don't have all eight, but they don't have seven either."

"Which would be true," Merrick said. "They abandoned some of the paintings when we first confronted them. Technically, physically, no, they cannot possess all eight."

"Is that good?" Chase asked hopefully.

"Hopefully they got all porn," Ollie said with a cheerful grin. His cheeks were rosy from the booze, and he sank down into his chair. He seemed sleepy, and his eyes were closing.

"Thanks for trying, kiddo," Chase said. "Anything else in the letters that you saw?"

"Hang on," Ollie complained, peeking open one eye and thumbing through his phone. "I mean, it's mostly this chick telling these dudes how they're gonna get all down and dirty when they get out of prison. And cult crap. Like, how much she wants to meet the gods."

"Anything about locations? Meeting places?"

"Only, like, body and butt places." Ollie yawned. "Sorry. There isn't much here."

Chase's phone beeped again, signaling another group of photographs from Milo. "Ah, maybe this will be more inspiring." He sent them to Ollie. "So, one of the other paintings we recovered was fake. This is a photo of a legit one that we found at Slappy's."

"We believe our suspect murdered Mr. Romero for the painting itself, but perhaps you will be able to discern something from the photo," Merrick said, studying Ollie's face. "That is, if you are feeling all right?"

"Oh, mm, I'm fine." Ollie tried to sit up a little straighter. "Just makes me sleepy, trying to do some of that crap."

"You should have 'em all now," Chase said after the last one had sent. "Check your messages, kiddo."

After sipping from his bottle, Ollie yawned again and leaned his head back as he scrolled through his phone. "Mm, I hope translating this crap helps. I mean, like, the world ending would be majorly bad."

"Very bad," Merrick agreed. "My brother is not well."

"What happened to you guys?" Chase asked suddenly. "I mean, you all just decided to take a nap, and then your brother goes nuts?"

"It is more complicated than that," Merrick said, tugging at his tie. "We went into the dreaming because mortals gave up our worship for others, like the Lord of Light and the Tauri deities in the far east. Year after year, bit by bit, we were all being forgotten. Great Azaethoth told us to fall into the dreaming and promised someday we would wake up to find a world that would love us again.

"It broke Salgumel's heart to leave all the mortals behind, no matter how we had been abandoned by them. He loved you all very much. He was angry with Great Azaethoth for forcing him to leave the kingdom of Aeon, and that anger twisted him. It turned his dreaming into a nightmare."

"A nightmare where the only possible solution is destroying it all and starting over from fuckin' scratch?" Chase concluded gravely.

"More or less." Merrick seemed troubled, and he bowed his head. "The best thing any of us can hope to do is ensure Salgumel remains in his slumber."

"Whatever happened to the Asra?" Ollie asked, his voice a little slurred. He blinked over at Merrick. "Does Beltara still have a whole bunch of them pulling her chariot?"

"Yes," Merrick replied with a soft smile. "Her Asra were loyal and followed her into the dreaming. Should she wake to ride the night skies, they rise with her."

Chase cleared his throat. "She's... who again?"

"Beltara, daughter of Zunnerath and Abigail the Starkiller," Merrick explained. "My father's half sister and my aunt. She's the goddess of insomnia, lost things, and falling stars. When you wish upon one, you're wishing to her."

"Her twin sister, Abeth, is the goddess of the written word, libraries, and wrote the first poem ever in godstongue," Ollie piped up cheerfully. "It was about her cat."

"They're the ones who ride around on the aurora borealis, right? Isn't there another sister?" Chase scratched his head, marveling at the weirdness of discussing a godly family tree with one of its members present.

"Common mistake," Merrick said. "Chandraleth is usually with them, yes, but she is actually Salgumel's spawn. She is my niece, therefore their grand-niece."

"Oh, right. Of course. Very common."

"Hey," Ollie hiccupped. "So, okay, zooming in on this picture of a picture really blows nuts, but I think I got something."

"What is it?" Chase asked quickly.

"A sacrifice of blessed blood in which many bright stars run rampant," Ollie read out loud. "Dressed upon a blade will break the veil, but only through death will he rise triumphant."

"Bright stars in the blood," Merrick mused. "It might be referring to someone who has starsight or someone who has starlight magic."

Chase grimaced. "Well, we now know why they're chopping out people's hearts."

"And why they have not been able to succeed," Merrick added. "The false painting must not have given them the correct specifications for the sacrifice. The passage suggests blood on a blade of some kind, not a heart. Also, neither Slappy nor the man killed at Mr. Martin's house were blessed with starsight."

"Sucks for anybody who has it," Ollie snorted. He made a face, scowling as he said, "You know, like *me*."

"You're safe," Chase promised. "We ain't said a word, okay? You don't have anything to worry about." He looked at Merrick. "Ol' Benjamin Merrick here is registered as divine, but uh, pity the fool who tries to come after him."

"Indeed." Merrick cracked a small smile.

"Okay, so," Ollie said briskly, his head bobbing forward, "if you guys don't need anything else, I'm so ready to pass out again. Sorry I didn't find the secret to saving the world or whatever."

"No problem, kiddo." Chase got up, and he hesitated on whether or not he should go in for a hug. He decided against it, settling for a firm pat on Ollie's shoulder instead. "Call me if you need anything, okay?"

Ollie lifted his head to smile wearily up at Chase. "I'm okay. I'm so okay."

Chase didn't believe him. He couldn't remember ever seeing his nephew this drained before, and he didn't know if it was from using his unique magic or the burden of carrying around so much heartache.

Whatever it was, Ollie was too damn young to look so old.

"Take care, kiddo," Chase said, heading to the door.

"Be kind to your body, young mortal," Merrick said politely as he followed after. "We are here if you need us."

"You got it, Wiggles." Ollie lifted himself up from the chair enough to provide the needed leverage to pivot face-first down into the couch.

Making sure the door was locked, Chase shut it behind them once they were out in the hall and sighed. "Huh. Fuck."

"What is the matter?" Merrick asked. "Worried about him?"

"Yeah, him and, like, a million other things," Chase replied. "Him translating everything hasn't gotten us jack shit, and there's still no sign of our boy Jeff. It's like they've all just disappeared. It's bullshit."

"Well, we know now they are interested in Class S magic users," Merrick said. "There are only a few registered in the entire state and maybe one or two in the whole city, so we can easily track down who the next potential target could be."

"I hate feeling like this. Like there's nothing we can do." Chase scrubbed his forehead. "It sucks."

"Well," Merrick mused, "if a certain someone had allowed me the proper time to track Mr. Martin's portal at the factory instead of interrogating me, perhaps we wouldn't be in this situation."

"Is that you making a joke?" Chase scoffed, laughing in spite of himself. "Because it's not funny."

"Made you smile," Merrick said with a pleased little grin. "I believe it was successful."

Chase felt his heart flutter, and he knew Merrick was doing his best to cheer him up. Before he could comment on how he appreciated those efforts, his phone rang. "It's forensics. Milo. Hold that thought."

"Hold it with what?"

"Hey, Detective Chase here," Chase said as he answered. "What's up, Milo?"

"Hey, listen. We got a big problem," Milo said hurriedly. "Daisy never looked into that damn prison letter thing, and now she's fucking disappeared on me, and it's her! It's fucking her!

"What?" Chase scowled. "Slow down, Milo! Her what?"

"The flower person on the letters is our flower! Daisy! She's the pen pal! She's totally in the cult!"

"Well, shit."

CHAPTER 10.

"SHE'S BEEN acting so damn weird since all of this started!" Milo went on, his voice nearly frantic now. "Like, way too happy kind of weird. I kept asking her to check out the letter shit, and she was totally brushing me off!"

"Where is she now?" Chase flipped the phone over to speaker as he and Merrick hurried back out to the car.

"I don't know!" Milo groaned. "Look, I turned my back for, like, two seconds, and she was gone. It's way too early for her to take lunch, but Officer Dancy says he saw her leaving."

"Try her cell?"

"Not picking up."

"Send her address. Fuckin' stat." Chase jumped into the passenger seat, scrambling to get his seat belt on before Merrick hauled ass out of the parking lot. "And you're sure it was her? Totally sure?"

"Yup," Milo confirmed. "Daisy Lopez. It's her. I even got copies of the visitors' log where she was seein' our buddy Jeff."

"Lovely."

"Address is coming at you. Good luck."

"Good work, Milo. Thanks." Chase hung up, waiting for the text to come through. "Okay, it's the Arbor Place neighborhood over by that new fancy grocery store they built, 565 Elm Lane."

"On it," Merrick said, narrowing his eyes as he hit the gas.

"I can't fuckin' believe it," Chase scoffed. "Sweet little Daisy is in a damn cult."

"Sweet little Daisy also has no respect for authority," Merrick pointed out.

"Is this about the donut thing?"

"It is a very clear departmental policy she chooses to violate most heinously. I am not surprised by her treachery."

"Well, let's just hope she hasn't made a run for it yet." Chase sighed. "If she really is tangled up with ol' Jeffy boy, they could be one portal jump away from vanishing forever."

"Not on my watch," Merrick growled, punching the accelerator again and zooming through traffic. Mysteriously, all the stoplights turned green, and they made it through the city in record time.

Daisy's neighborhood was quaint and modest, and Chase was relieved to see her car still in the driveway as they pulled up.

"All right, let's go," Chase urged.

"Wait." Merrick reached over and touched Chase's forehead. "This will help."

"What did you do?" Chase wrinkled his nose. "Feels tingly."

"A truth spell," Merrick explained. "And yes, before you ask, the same kind of truth spell that requires a suspect's consent and we need a judge's order to cast."

"Desperate times and all that."

"She may have information we need to prevent the end of the world. Yes, I would say it is very desperate."

Together they marched up to Daisy's front door, and Chase rang the bell. He heard movement inside, and he tensed as he prepared himself for anything.

Jeff Martin or another horde of cultists could be in there. Hell, they could have some fucked-up monster from another world or even their own god, since those guys seemed to be running around all over this place.

The door opened, fortunately revealing only Daisy in a bathrobe and brightly colored bunny slippers.

"Oh, uh, hi," Daisy squeaked, immediately recoiling from the door. "Detectives, uh, what a nice surprise! I was just taking a nap. Uh. What are you doing here?"

"We know you were the one sending letters to Slappy and Jeff," Chase declared boldly. "We also know that you're mixed up in this fuckin' Salgumel cult. So start talking. Right now."

"Shit." Daisy's eyes bugged out. "Am I under arrest?"

"Not yet. Depends on how cooperative you are." Chase clicked his tongue. "Ditching work ain't a real good look."

"I'm sorry! I was having a bad day, and I really needed to take some personal time, but, uh, I see what you mean." Daisy tightened her robe around herself and gestured for them to come in. "I'll talk to you guys, okay?"

That felt like the truth, so at least the spell seemed to be working.

They gathered in Daisy's cluttered living room, and she flitted around picking up laundry and trash to free up the furniture.

"I'm sorry it's such a mess," she said. "Please, uh, sit down. Do you guys want some coffee or something?"

"No, we're good." Chase took one of the cleared spots on the sofa, but Merrick chose to remain standing. "Start talking. Now."

"Slappy Romero is my ex-boyfriend," Daisy confessed, sinking down on the other end of the couch. "Jeff Martin is also my ex-boyfriend, but uh, much more recently. As in, like today."

"You met them through the prison pen pal program, right?"

"Jeff, yes, but I was dating Slappy before he got arrested. We had met at a Urilitha party a few years ago, and well, we hit it off really well, and we ended up joining a coven dedicated to Salgumel together."

"You mean the charming guys that tried to gun us down at the shoe factory?" Chase raised his brows. "The cult?"

"It wasn't a cult then!" Daisy protested, her defiance faltering. "It was just... it was just some Sages hanging out with other Sages. It used to be really nice."

"So, more magical fun times and less murder?" Chase drawled.

"Hey! That's not funny!" Daisy yelped. "I didn't know any of that stuff was going to happen!"

A lie.

"Come on, Daisy," Chase snorted. "You've been in this coven for a while, probably had lots of fun little parties. You had to know they were up to something."

"Please, you've gotta believe me. I didn't want anyone to get hurt," Daisy mewled pitifully. "I thought Jeff would just take the painting and leave!"

"So Jeff got the house key from you?" Chase accused. "Is that how he got in?"

"Yes," Daisy confirmed, wiping tears from her eyes. "Slappy had given it to me back when we were dating. You know, before he went to prison for the whole fraud thing."

Truth.

"He was so handsome. He had the nicest beard." Daisy smiled sadly as she went on. "I always used to tell him that I couldn't wait to run my fingers through it again."

Partially true.

"So what happened? He goes to jail, you're still in love with his awesome beard, and then what?"

"After he got out of prison, I was supposed to come stay with him for a big romantic weekend to celebrate. I was so excited because I hadn't seen him in weeks. He hated when I visited him in jail, so I didn't see him much. Well, he called me when I was on my way there to say he wanted the key back and that his ex-girlfriend was coming over."

"Ouch."

Dick move on Slappy's part and also the truth.

"I never gave the stupid key back." Daisy shook her head. "I didn't want to ever see him again."

A lie. She definitely had wanted to see him again, and Chase felt a faint twinge of pity.

"Slappy left the coven after we broke up, and then I met Jeff through the pen pal program. He was a very devout Salgumel worshipper, and he joined the coven as soon as he got out of prison. He's the one who told us all about Lord Collins and the paintings.

"When he found out Slappy had one of them at his gallery, he started asking me all of these questions. He knew me and Slappy used to date, and well, I maybe might have told him that I still had a key to Slappy's place, but I didn't think it mattered then."

"Lemme guess. You guys didn't know the one at Slappy's gallery was a fake?"

"No. The coven didn't find out until I examined the painting after it got left behind at the factory, and I... I told them. Jeff realized Slappy must have been keeping the real painting at his house, and he remembered that I still had a key."

"So, after you tell your little boyfriend Jeff all about it, you hand over the house key you just happened to still have? Is this before or after he carved his buddy's heart out of his chest?"

"Look," Daisy protested, "I'm a Sage. Do you have any idea how incredible it was to find a guy who shared my beliefs? After Slappy broke my heart, I didn't think I'd ever find anyone ever again! But then I met Jeff, and it was just… it was just so magical!"

"Answer the question," Merrick said coldly.

"After the heart thing." Daisy stared down at her hands. "I love him, and I love the gods. It… it felt like the right thing to do. He told me Louis had been a willing sacrifice, but it didn't work, and they didn't know why. They needed the real painting for the ritual, and he promised me that he wasn't going to hurt Slappy."

"Where is Jeff now?" Chase demanded. "Where is the rest of the cult hiding out?"

"I don't know!" Daisy cried. "Look, Jeff has pretty much taken over the coven now, and he started to push me out. He didn't want me to get too involved. I had no idea he was even capable of something like this."

"Why didn't you tell us the truth?" Chase scowled. "You realize by giving your little boyfriend that key, you could be looking at accessory to murder, right? You should have told us what was going on the fucking second you—"

"I didn't think you guys would believe me!" Daisy burst into tears. "I'm a Sage! Everybody thinks we're crazy and we're all a bunch of rogue witches! You're probably using a truth spell on me right now! I didn't want anyone to get hurt! I just, I just wanted to help!"

"Help who?"

"The gods! I want them to come back so badly! If Salgumel wakes up, he'll bring them all back. Don't you understand?" She sniffled, wiping her nose on her sleeve. "When I first got involved in the coven, it was all about reconnecting with Salgumel. Now it's gotten so out of control with this ritual thing, and all these poor people are dying…." She began to cry again.

"Like your friend Louis? Like Slappy?" Chase pushed. "How many more people are gonna die, Daisy?"

"I'm sorry," she sobbed. "I should have said something after he killed Lou. I should have…. Jeff said he was willing, that he wanted to do it, but now I don't know! I'm so sorry."

That was the truth, but Chase couldn't help but wonder what she was sorry for. It was possible to manipulate a truth spell with carefully selected answers, but seeing her look so genuinely upset made him feel like a jerk for doubting her.

Even so, there was a knot in his stomach telling him this was all wrong somehow.

"I can understand the desire to reconnect with the gods," Merrick spoke up, offering her a surprisingly sympathetic smile. "They have been away for so long, and the faithful that are left are ridiculed and isolated. However, what your cult seeks would have very devastating consequences."

"You mean because everyone believes Salgumel has gone mad?" Daisy sniffed. "I don't believe that." She noisily snorted back more tears. "I know what the coven is doing is wrong, but Salgumel just needs to see that people still care about him and the other gods. When he wakes up, he will reward all of the faithful."

"I'm sorry, Daisy, but trust me when I say that's not going to happen," Merrick said. "We must leave Salgumel sleeping. It's for the best."

"How the hell would you know?" Daisy spat with unexpected venom, crossing her arms angrily. "You're Lucian. You couldn't possibly understand how much this hurts!"

Chase saw how those words hurt Merrick, and he thought he might be about to show off a tentacle or two to comfort Daisy.

Merrick said nothing, and he turned away.

"All right, look here, Daisy. Do you know anything else about the coven that could help us?" Chase asked. "Where they might be? What they're planning next?"

"I know they won't stop until it's done," Daisy said softly. "I know they're close. The last thing Jeff told me is that they only need one last ingredient to power the ritual."

Yeah, and the missing ingredient is another fuckin' human sacrifice.

"When was the last time you saw Jeff?"

"This morning before I went in to work," she replied firmly. "I told him I was breaking up with him and leaving the coven."

"After all those years? You'd just give it all up?"

"I don't want to be a part of anyone else getting hurt," Daisy said. "I still believe Salgumel will come back to us, one way or another, but I don't want it to be like this. I can't be a part of all of this death, okay?"

"You know we're gonna have to report you," Chase warned. "You withheld evidence, shared private information, and compromised our entire investigation."

"I know." Daisy bowed her head. "I knew you guys were gonna find out eventually. It's why I left work today. I couldn't keep pretending everything was gonna be okay, not with Milo pushing me about the letters. I know… I know my life is over now. I lost my boyfriend, lost my coven, and I'm probably gonna lose my job."

"You can get a new boyfriend, preferably one that's not into cults or crime, and you can find a new job," Chase promised. "You coming clean with us counts for a lot. What they do to you is gonna be up to internal affairs, but I'll talk to the captain for you, okay?"

"You'd do that?" Daisy stared at him. "After lying and, and everything else I did?"

"People do crazy shit for the people they love, gods included," Chase said, glancing at Merrick with a fleeting smile. "Just sit tight, and we'll see what we can do."

"Thank you, Chase," Daisy gushed. "Thank you both so much. I swear I'll tell you anything else if I think it's important! Really!"

"Take care of yourself, kiddo," Chase said as he stood up. "You hear from Jeffy boy, you give us a call, okay?"

"Okay. Thank you so much!"

They left Daisy tearful but hopeful, and they sat in the car for several long moments before either one of them spoke.

"I do not believe her." Merrick drummed his fingers along the steering wheel. "I think she is lying to us. She should be incarcerated at once."

"The only big thing she lied about was not wanting to see Slappy again," Chase said grimly. "I don't know. The whole waterworks deal, the poor girl getting swept up in a bad group of people bit…."

"It is very plausible, but I still do not believe her."

"I fuckin' agree ten thousand percent. I feel like she played us, but I can't prove it."

"We could still procure a warrant for her arrest."

"Yeah, what for? She's just gonna get placed on administrative leave while they conduct their big ol' fancy internal investigation." Chase rubbed his forehead. "And we're still no fucking closer to finding these cult assholes."

"At least we know how Mr. Martin was able to enter Mr. Romero's residence to murder him."

"Yeah, 'cause that's real helpful right now."

"Perhaps we should contact my nephew and Mr. Beaumont." Merrick closed his eyes. "It is possible they have had more luck than we have."

"Sure." Chase got out his phone and prepared to dial. "We still gotta call in and report what little Miss Daisy has been up to. The captain is gonna fuckin' freak."

His phone rang.

"That should be Sloane," Merrick said. "I am sorry. I told Loch it was urgent."

"Wait, how did you…? Never mind." Chase cleared his throat, answering the phone on speaker. "Detectives Chase and Merrick here."

"Hey, it's Sloane," Sloane greeted. "Loch told me he got a message from Gordoth and wanted us to call?"

"Yeah, we've had a little bit of a situation develop on our end, and we were hoping that maybe you guys had managed to turn something up about this cultist bullshit."

"What's going on?"

"It's our forensic tech, Daisy Lopez," Chase replied. "She's apparently very into bad boys who like Salgumel and have awful names like Slappy and Jeff."

"Huh?"

Chase caught Sloane up on what had happened since they'd last spoken, concluding, "So now, if I'm counting right, they've gotten their hands on anywhere between five and seven of the eight paintings that can end the world."

"The most they could have had was five," Sloane said. "I asked around, and a very close friend of ours was hired to steal some paintings last year. Their contact was a guy named Jeff."

"Oh really?" Chase glanced over to Merrick. That certainly lined up with Ollie's reading. "What happened?"

"They tried to kill him instead of paying him, and he torched at least two of the paintings. This same friend may have also been responsible for the auction theft."

"And that painting?"

"Also destroyed. So that's good, right? This means they don't have enough info to conduct the ritual?"

"Our girl Daisy says all they're waiting on is the last ingredient. Whatever your friend destroyed, I guess it was more porn they didn't need."

"Well, shit."

"One way or another, they've got everything for the ritual except this human sacrifice bit. Ollie was able to translate Slappy's painting from a photo, and it says they need someone with bright stars in their blood."

"So, someone with starlight magic or that's been blessed by starsight?"

"Exactly so," Merrick confirmed. "Such individuals are quite rare, but the cultists will certainly be searching for them. That includes my mortal vessel, Benjamin Merrick."

"And you too, Sloane," Chase added.

"I know," Sloane said. "Don't worry. I'll be extra careful. And hey, we thought of a few places that the cultists might be using to meet at. Can't have dastardly secret meetings without a place to meet up for drinks and snacks, right? We'll check 'em out and see if anything turns up."

"Like where?" Chase demanded. "You two can't just go galivanting off playing cops, you know. Give us the locations, and we'll go."

"Uh, yeah, I can. I'm a licensed private investigator!" Sloane countered. "Besides, do you really think you guys could walk into a place like Dead to Rites and get anyone to talk to you?"

"Dead to Rites?" Merrick wrinkled his nose. "That nasty little bar by the old church downtown?"

"Yes! That's the one," Loch's voice chimed in cheerfully. "I've heard they have their very own shrine dedicated to me."

"It is a veritable cesspool of criminal activity."

"And they have a shrine! To me!" Loch sounded very pleased. "We are going to investigate, and I am going to have a *daiquiri*."

"Rites is owned by Sages," Sloane said. "Maybe some of the cultists have been hanging out there, maybe even trying to recruit new members. It's a good place to start anyway. We'll call if we get anything."

"Be safe," Chase cautioned.

"As if I would let anything happen to my beloved mate while he's carrying our child!" Loch scoffed.

"Talk to you later, guys," Sloane said.

"Bye." Chase hung up and slumped in his seat. "I'm sure this is fine. A god and a pregnant witch walking into a seedy bar looking for criminals. Totally fine."

"Azzath will take care of his mate and their child," Merrick soothed, leaving Daisy's neighborhood and heading back to the station. "Fear not."

"Fear not, my ass, we're right back to square one again," Chase complained. "And I still have no idea—" He stopped himself, having been about to joke that he didn't know what Merrick wanted for dinner.

"What?"

"Don't worry about it. Nothing that can't wait." Chase cleared his throat. "We should check back in at the precinct, let the captain and everybody know what's going on."

Merrick was quiet for a few moments before saying carefully, "I would like to amend my earlier decision and offer you a compromise."

"Huh?"

"As long as we are alone in the vehicle together, we can have conversations including but not limited to relationship topics such as dinner."

"Merry, really, we don't have to do that—"

"You're not the only one who wants to talk about it," Merrick said passionately. "I want to talk to you about everything. About food, films, what color socks you prefer! What your dreams are, what places you want to travel to!

"I see now that denying ourselves only hurts us both, because my superior professionalism comes across as some sort of cold apathy when, in fact, I want this just as much as you do. Perhaps even more because I have never shared it with anyone else before."

"I'll follow your lead," Chase said reassuringly, surprised and touched by Merrick's sudden outburst of emotion. "Whatever you wanna do, I'm all fuckin' for it. I love you. Just the chance to be with you is more than I ever thought I would have."

Merrick looked a little embarrassed, perhaps from getting so worked up, but he was smiling. He glanced over to Chase, bravely stretching out a tentacle to take his hand. "Right now, I would like to discuss dinner."

"We can totally do that." Chase gave Merrick's tentacle a tender squeeze. "And oh, just for the record," he teased, "using words like 'superior professionalism' is much more hurtful than not wanting to talk about dinner."

"Noted."

"Now, how about you tell me how you feel about Bolognese sauce?"

"I will do my best to express myself thoroughly."

They stayed that way, tentacle and hand curled together, chatting about food and movies until they arrived back at the precinct.

Merrick gave Chase's hand one last tug before letting go, parking the car, and smiling shyly. "So. I believe we are settled on pasta and frozen garlic breadsticks for this evening?"

"Sounds good to me," Chase confirmed. "I'm still down to watch all three *Die Hard* movies if you really want."

"We can skip the second one."

"Ugh, I love you so much."

Merrick laughed, clearing his throat and trying to resume his usual stoic demeanor. "We still have a lot of work left to do. We are both going to have to write full statements on what happened with Daisy and file our reports with the captain before the day is out."

"Yeah, and passing along Ollie's translations to Milo might not be a bad idea. He's a smart kid. Maybe he'll figure something out we haven't seen yet. He's all up-to-date with this godly business after all."

"An excellent suggestion."

"I have those from time to time," Chase said with a tip of his hat.

"I would also like to make a suggestion," Merrick said casually. "After work, we will report to our homes to prepare for an evening together. I will come over to your home at seven o'clock, enjoy the delicious meal you're going to prepare, and then I would like to take all of your clothes off."

"That's... that's a very good suggestion," Chase stuttered, his cheeks pinking up. "Ah, is the clothes-off bit happening before or after the *Die Hard* marathon?"

"After." Merrick paused. "Or at least until I can no longer keep my hands off of you."

"Good to know. Just checking."

The end of their shift could not come soon enough. Despite the constant walls they were hitting with the case and the constant threat of apocalyptic forces hanging over their heads, Chase was in a really good damn mood.

Tonight he had a dinner date with the god he loved.

CHAPTER 11.

DAISY LOPEZ was immediately placed on leave pending an internal investigation, and Chase and Merrick both filed their statements and had them on the captain's desk by lunch. Milo was grateful for Ollie's translations and promised to keep them updated. Sloane called to check in but unfortunately had nothing new to share.

Other than that Loch was very disappointed in the quality of his shrine.

Merrick and Chase hit the streets to follow up on some of Jeff Martin's previous addresses, his acquaintances, and even his dentist. They tried tracking down some of the other cultists that Milo had been able to identify and still nothing.

By the time their shift was finally over, Chase was exhausted and frustrated.

"Ready, partner?" Merrick said in what was probably his best attempt to sound casual despite the big smile on his face.

"Yeah," Chase said, immediately perking up. He could be tired later. He had a date to prepare for. He frowned when he saw a big box of files in Merrick's hands. "What's that?"

"Some light reading," Merrick replied.

"A giant box of files is light reading?"

"It's everything we have on Slappy Romero, Jeff Martin, and their known criminal associates." Merrick fidgeted. "I thought perhaps we could look through them again tonight."

Chase honestly didn't know if Merrick was being serious or if this was meant to be some sort of cover to deflect gossip. "Uh, yeah. Of course."

"Good." Merrick held his head high. "Then I will see you tonight. To go over these files."

"You got it." Chase resisted the urge to laugh, walking Merrick outside and parting ways in the parking lot. He still had to hit up the grocery store to get what he needed for dinner and maybe try to clean up a bit.

Okay, clean up a lot.

He knew he had nothing to eat at home, so he got all the ingredients for the meal, including a box of frozen garlic breadsticks. He opted for wine instead of beer, and he wondered if a god could get drunk.

Better get a few bottles, just in case.

After paying and packing the food away in the car, he hurried home to get ready. He put the cold ingredients up, cleared the sink, and ran the dishwasher for the first time in weeks. He swept and wiped down the counters before turning his attention to the living room.

It was still clean from the last time Merrick was here and had magically swept everything away, but Chase decided to dig some old bottles and trash out from beneath the sofa that had escaped the godly purge.

By the time he'd changed the sheets and made the bed, it was almost seven.

Fuck, when did he get so sweaty?

He took the fastest shower of his life, then jumped into a pair of sweats and a T-shirt because of course he didn't have anything else clean to wear except his damn suits.

Sweeping his damp hair up into a knot, he hurried into the kitchen to start cooking. As he was pulling out the pots he needed, the entire contents of the cabinet decided to come tumbling out in a violent crash.

"Shit!"

He cringed at the noise and took a deep breath. His damn hands were shaking.

"Calm the fuck down," he scolded. "It's just dinner. Just fuckin' dinner. Dinner for the man you're madly in love with. Who is also a god… and now you're talking to yourself. Fuck."

Chase went for the wine, taking a sip right from the bottle to hopefully calm his nerves. He couldn't recall the last time he'd been this jittery over a date. He never got nervous over stuff like this, not ever.

Merrick had been by his place before, but this time was different. It was the first time he was coming over as more than his partner, and Chase wanted it to be perfect.

He cleaned up the mess of pots and pans except the ones he needed, nearly jumping out of his skin when he heard a knock at the door.

After another big gulp of wine for courage, he went to answer it.

Merrick was waiting on the other side with a bottle of scotch in his hand and a dazzling smile on his face. He stared openly at Chase, stammering, "W-wow. You look wonderful."

"Thanks." Chase blushed, taking in Merrick's snug blue polo shirt and fitted jeans. "You too. You look awesome." He stepped back from the door. "Come on in."

"Thank you."

Chase wanted to kiss him. He'd been thinking about it all day when he wasn't occupied by physical descriptions and fingerprint analysis and worrying about the world ending. Even though they'd literally been by each other's side for the entire shift, it seemed like they'd been apart for ages, and all he wanted to do now was touch.

Despite his desire, he felt awkward, and he wasn't sure if he should make a move.

Would that somehow be disrespectful to an all-powerful god?

He settled on leaning in to kiss Merrick's cheek, and the bashful grin it earned him let him know it was a good choice.

"Um." Merrick quickly presented Chase with the bottle. "Here. This is for you."

"Wow, thanks. I had gotten some wine, but this is…." Chase paused as he read the label. "This is Honey Shepard's scotch."

"Yes."

"This stuff is aged for, like, fifty years and costs, like, a couple grand a pop. How the hell can you afford this?"

"As a god, I have very few needs, so Merrick's paychecks tend to gather in his account." Merrick frowned. "Do you not like it? You seem to know a lot about it."

"It just… wow. Beats the hell out of my shitty grocery store wine!" Chase laughed, walking into the kitchen. "We are definitely drinking this."

"I am glad you are pleased." Merrick stopped short, frozen in place as he looked around the apartment. "Oh!"

"What?"

"You cleaned," Merrick said, not even attempting to hide his shock.

"Yeah, well. I picked up a little." Chase shrugged. He managed to find two clean glasses to pour the scotch in, although one was a bat coffee mug and the other was a plastic fast-food cup he kept reusing.

"This is more than a little." Merrick pressed into Chase's space and chastely kissed his cheek. "I appreciate the effort. It's very thoughtful."

"No big deal." Chase beamed, his chest swelling with pride. The kiss made his heart stumble over itself, and he hastily cleared his throat. "So, uh, you want the bat or the Burger Gal cup?"

"I suppose the bat is appropriate."

"Here." Chase opened the scotch and poured them some, offering the bat mug. "You never did say what you look like. Is it like that?"

Merrick made a face at the cartoonish bat leering from the side of the cup. "Close enough."

"You know I could probably use my phone and look it up." Chase pulled out butter and cream from the fridge. "The internet is pretty useful, you know."

"I do not want you to know what I look like yet."

"You really think I'm gonna judge you?" Chase took a small sip. And then another.

Damn, that was smooth.

"I do not think you would intentionally be cruel, but yes, I do believe you would find my godly form unpleasant."

"I don't think my body is that pleasant either," Chase reminded him. He set his cup down and placed a pan on the stove, cranking up the dial for the heat. "Just about everybody has some hang-ups about their looks."

"I do not know why you do. I think you are quite beautiful." Merrick stepped a little closer and gently placed his hand on Chase's shoulder.

Smiling, Chase shook his head. "I'd gladly take bat wings over stretch marks and this extra fifty pounds I've been trying to lose since the nineties. I mean, if you even have those. The wings, I mean."

"What if I did?"

"Well, I'd love those too." Chase kissed him. It was soft, sweet, and he wrapped his arms around Merrick and pulled him against his chest.

Merrick gasped before melting in Chase's arms, and he ran his fingers up into his hair. Thwarted by the bun, he mumbled, "I like your hair when it is accessible."

"Totally easy fix." Chase quickly undid the bun, groaning as Merrick dove into his wet hair to scratch at his scalp. He kissed him again, and their lips glided together until Chase was out of breath.

"Your… your pan is probably hot by now." Merrick's eyes had turned into black pools sparkling with stars, and he was smiling as they parted. "I did not mean to get so carried away."

"Baby boy, you can carry me anywhere you wanna fuckin' go," Chase promised. He turned away to very casually adjust his thickening cock, clearing his throat. "But uh, it's hard to have dinner together if I don't make it."

"Of course." Merrick retreated back a few steps.

Chase put a stick of butter in the pan to melt while he minced some garlic. "You, uh…." He struggled to think of something to talk about that wasn't related to work. "You like scotch?"

"I know you do." Merrick smiled. "Mortal libations do not affect me."

"Right." Chase stopped chopping for a moment. "I mean, does anything?"

"What?"

"Affect you. Like, can anything hurt you?"

"Nothing mortal." Merrick shrugged. "We gods can kill each other, but the damage must be quite extreme. Decapitation is very effective."

"Ouch."

"I can only assume. I have never had my head removed."

"Good. I like it right where it is." Chase added the garlic to the butter, and he grabbed a pot to fill with water for the pasta. He poured some salt in and then took another drink of the delicious scotch, and it prompted him to ask, "You don't buy anything for yourself? Nothing?"

"I pay Merrick's bills, donate a percentage to charity, and allow the rest to accrue interest. I do not require much, as I have said."

"Huh. I guess you would save a ton of money not eating." Chase paused to think about where a lot of his own money went and added, "Or drinking."

"It can be quite expensive."

"Who you tellin'?" Chase reached for a small carton of cream, then added it to the saucepan with a sprinkle of black pepper and onion powder. He noticed Merrick's forehead was wrinkling up, prompting him to ask, "You okay?"

"I am sorry. I am distracted."

"The case?" Chase drank the rest of his scotch, repressing a greedy moan at the awesome flavor. "What is it? We got fuck all in column A and fuck nothing in column B."

"I do not know what these columns are, but yes, I agree we have nothing." Merrick glanced at the scotch and took a dainty sip. "I still do not trust that Daisy was honest with us."

"Maybe we can take another crack at her later." Chase dropped the pasta into the boiling water. "The way she just happened to suddenly leave work like that? She was probably waiting for us."

"She was expecting to be interrogated?"

"Would explain how she was able to beat a truth spell. She already knew what she was gonna say." Chase stirred the sauce and began to work in scoops of grated Parmesan cheese.

Merrick tiptoed closer to the stove, watching Chase curiously. "It is certainly possible."

"I still can't believe we can't find these dudes. It's like they've disappeared." Chase turned on the oven to preheat for the breadsticks and gave the sauce another stir to keep the cheese from clumping. He noticed Merrick staring and teased, "What? You never seen anyone cook before?"

"I have never seen *you* cook before." Merrick smiled and took a polite step away to refill their glasses. "My intention is not to make you feel uncomfortable."

"It's fine." Chase accepted his newly filled glass, turning to rest his hand on Merrick's hip. "You can watch me cook all you want."

Merrick leaned into Chase's touch, his smile growing. "It suits you." He kissed his cheek. "It also smells wonderful."

"Gimme, like, fifteen more minutes and it'll be ready."

"I cannot wait."

It was closer to thirty minutes by the time Chase was done because he kept getting distracted by Merrick. Having him close made it too tempting to resist stealing kisses and little touches. What was an innocent smooch turned into a heated up make-out session that ended with Chase pushed against the counter and nearly burning the breadsticks.

Dinner was served, their hands mostly stayed to themselves, and they ate together on the sofa, watching the first movie. Chase finished his plate and went back for more, much more relaxed now despite his earlier nerves.

The scotch helped.

Though the heat between him and Merrick had been reduced to a simmer, Chase knew it wouldn't take much to crank it back up. The anticipation of what was to come was thrilling, and he was excited.

Not that he was expecting anything in particular to happen. He didn't want to pressure Merrick, and he didn't mind waiting.

Even if it felt like Merrick was about to pounce on him at any second.

Maybe it was just Chase's imagination.

"You get enough to eat?" Chase asked, stacking his empty plate on top of Merrick's on the coffee table. He leaned back, stretching his arms along the back of the couch.

"Yes," Merrick replied, settling in against Chase's side.

Chase slowly wrapped his arm around Merrick's shoulders. "This okay?"

"Very much okay." Merrick smiled up at him.

Chase couldn't stop looking at Merrick's lips, unconsciously leaning in. "I can get you more if you want."

"No, thank you." Merrick reached up to stroke Chase's beard, eyeing his mouth as well. "It was delicious, and I am quite satisfied."

"Are you?" Chase's heart fluttered. It felt hotter in here now, and they were almost close enough to kiss.

"Well…." Merrick boldly dragged his hand down Chase's broad chest. "There may be some other ways in which I would not mind being satisfied."

"Oh really?"

"Without a doubt."

"I'd be a pretty terrible host if I didn't help you out." Chase squeezed Merrick's shoulder. "How about I work on satisfying you in some of those other ways?"

"I… I would like that," Merrick said, his voice a bit breathless. He surged forward to kiss Chase, passionate and sweet, desperately fisting his hand into his shirt.

Chase tried to get him to slow down, but Merrick was far too eager. He gave in, letting Merrick kiss him as hard as he wanted to. He gasped as Merrick suddenly pushed him down on the couch and crawled on top of him.

Merrick's tentacles were out, a few curling around Chase's arms and another hugging his thigh. He was touching Chase all over, and he was kissing him so fiercely and fast that their teeth clicked.

The grinding of Merrick's body was spectacular, and Chase could do nothing to hide how hard he was. Judging by the way Merrick zeroed in on his cock and pressed down, he could definitely feel it.

Chase hated how close he was already, and he didn't want things to end this soon. Even with a god who could literally make him orgasm over and over without end, he still had his pride to consider.

Grabbing Merrick's hips, Chase urged him to slow down. "Hey, hey, easy. Keep that up and this is gonna be over quick."

"Is this wrong?" Merrick asked, cringing in embarrassment as he pulled away. "I do not know what I am doing."

"That's okay." Chase kissed his cheek soothingly. "Neither do I. Not like this, I mean. There's no need to rush, okay? Just tell me what you want to do, and we'll do it."

"I want...." Merrick's gaze grew dark. "I very much want to be inside of you."

Chase could feel his eyes trying to bulge out of his head, and he struggled to rein in his emotions. "Yeah, we, we can definitely do that."

"Yes? I was not... sure...." Merrick trailed off, looking positively sheepish.

"What?" Chase snorted. "You think because I'm a big ol' bastard that I wouldn't, ahem, want you inside me?"

"I did not know the proper way to inquire about your... preferences."

"You just gotta ask," Chase soothed, "but I'll save you the trouble by telling you I am one hundred and ten percent down with you being all up in me, okay?"

"You cannot technically have more than a hundred percent." Merrick fidgeted. "But I understand that is hyperbole emphasizing a positive response?"

"Absolutely." Chase rubbed Merrick's hips. "We ain't gotta jump right in, though. We got all night, okay?"

"I am afraid I am a bit impatient."

"No shit." Chase chuckled. He patted Merrick's hips again, sliding his hands up his back. "Let's start off by gettin' into bed. Don't wanna have your first time on my nasty-ass couch."

"The location is irrelevant, but I can see how a bed would be more appropriate."

"Come on." Chase urged Merrick to get off him and led him by the hand into his bedroom. They got into bed together, and Chase found himself on his back with Merrick on top of him again.

"May I remove your clothing, Elwood?" Merrick asked politely.

"Yeah, I can—" Chase had grabbed the bottom of his shirt to pull it off, but there was no need. All of his clothes had simply vanished. "Okay, that works."

Merrick sat back on Chase's hips, rubbing his hands worshipfully over his round belly. He traced all the silvery lines that Chase despised, and he smiled as he said, "You are so beautiful."

"You need your head examined," Chase teased, trying to grin but soon faltering. He was totally exposed, and his body was torn between shame for its appearance and the arousal brewing from Merrick's attention.

He was turning shades of red he didn't think were humanly possible from the conflicting combination.

"I do not think so." Merrick slid his hands higher, squeezing Chase's pecs and working his thumbs over his nipples. He continued to play until each one was hard, and he looked especially pleased with himself.

"Just throwing this out there—" Chase cleared his throat, already breathless. "—but it's only fair if we're both naked."

"You are deflecting."

"Yes, yes, I am. But I'm also telling the truth."

"Very well." Merrick tilted his head, and his clothes disappeared. "There, are you happy?"

"Uh-huh." Chase beckoned Merrick down for a kiss, and he wrapped his thick arms around his shoulders. He groaned quietly as they kissed, shifting his legs apart as Merrick settled between his thighs.

"I... I can get you ready for me," Merrick panted. He sounded nervous. "If, if you are ready, that is."

"Baby boy, for you, always," Chase promised with another kiss, spreading his legs wide. He kept his focus on Merrick's lips, ignoring the cringing thoughts of how much thicker his thighs were than Merrick's or how his stomach felt so much bigger as they rubbed together.

None of that mattered. It shouldn't. Merrick loved him, curves and all.

Chase's ass suddenly felt wet, and there was a new pressure from within. He was being stretched without a single touch from either tentacle or hand. It was weird, kinda hot, and Chase let out a quiet moan.

"Does that... feel good?" Merrick asked, kissing Chase's beard and nuzzling his cheek.

"Yeah. Weird, but good. Really good." Chase ran his fingers down Merrick's shoulders, taking a deep breath as the pressure grew, flirting now with discomfort. "Mm, easy."

"My apologies," Merrick murmured, the pressure backing off immediately. "I want to make sure you are prepared properly."

"What exactly are you, uh, preparing me for?"

"Whatever you are willing to take."

Chase took another deep breath to steel himself for what was to come. He'd seen what Merrick was working with, and wow, it was a lot.

The four givey-takey tentacles were already very intimidating, but those tentacle-cocks were in a class of their own. It was going to be equivalent to having his own personal orgy, and he was excited and already tingling with adrenaline.

The challenge of pushing his body to its limits making love to a god was one that he simply could not refuse.

"Bring it on," Chase said firmly.

Merrick smiled in reply, and he leaned down to kiss Chase. More of his tentacles unfurled from his back, curling around Chase and holding him close, gently spreading his legs.

Chase kissed back passionately, groaning when he felt the first tease of a tentacle at his hole. The heat was pleasant, and he let out a very satisfied sound as the tentacle began to push inside of him. "Merry...."

"Elwood, I am... I am inside of you." Merrick's voice was a frantic whisper, and he moaned as his tentacle pushed in deeper. "By Great Azaethoth's horns... you feel... you feel incredible...."

"So do you. Fuck, so do you." Chase clung to Merrick, dragging his nails down his back as the tentacle thrust. It was erratic at first, clumsy, and Chase rolled his hips down to help set a steady pace. "Come on, baby... like that... just like that."

"Oh, Elwood... I am so sorry... I am...!" Merrick cried out, shoving his face down into Chase's chest as he suddenly came. "Ah, *fuck*!"

"Merr!" Chase gasped as he felt a rush of intense warmth inside him, pulse after pulse of thick come leaving him full and heavy. Even excited as he was, it wasn't enough to push him over the edge to come himself, but damn if it hadn't felt good.

Merrick withdrew the tentacle with a low whine, turning his head away in shame. "I am so very sorry. That... that was very unexpected. I did not mean—"

"Hey, hey, Merry!" Chase did his best to be reassuring even as he felt Merrick's godly load leaking out of him, and all he wanted to do was beg for more. "It's okay. It happens. It's actually a compliment."

"Surely you jest."

"Look at me." Chase turned Merrick's face toward him. "It's totally okay, and it's very much a compliment. Kinda nice knowing I could make a god lose control."

"Your body... you... you brought much more pleasure than I was expecting," Merrick confessed, leaning into Chase's palm. He still looked embarrassed, but he was smiling now.

"That's what I'm talkin' about." Chase grinned. "And hey, we still got what, five more of those bad boys to play with, right?"

"If you still desire me...."

"Oh, without a doubt," Chase swore, chuckling lightly as he pulled Merrick in for a much-needed kiss. "Mmm. So, does this mean you're still the Untouched?"

"No." Merrick laughed. "I should think not."

CHAPTER 12.

THE KISS quickly reignited their passion, and it wasn't long before Chase felt a new tentacle pressing inside his body. Everything was slicker now, and the thick appendage slid in without any resistance. It seemed to go on and on, and he couldn't stop moaning.

It was beyond fantastic to be this full, and Chase let himself get loud. He wanted Merrick to know how much he was enjoying himself, and he eagerly rocked his body down to help keep him on rhythm.

Merrick followed the direction well, thrusting his tentacle deep and slow. He was making the most delightful little sounds: small gasps of surprise, delighted moans, and low growls that sent a shiver down Chase's spine.

"This is better, yes?"

"Mmm, good," Chase grunted. "So good."

"Is the depth adequate?"

"Oh, yeah, yup, definitely."

"Is this a satisfactory speed?"

"Ohhh, yeah."

"Are you certain?" Merrick sounded tense.

"Merr… just… come on. Just do it. Don't think about it. Just fuck me." Chase's body was so open, his hole sopping wet, and he dragged his teeth down Merrick's jaw. "Come on… I can take more. Come on, Merry. Show me what you can do."

Merrick shuddered, turning his head to catch Chase's lips in another fierce kiss. "I do not wish to hurt you."

"Come on," Chase urged, trying to stretch his legs farther apart. "Give it to me, Merr. Please."

Groaning loudly, Merrick sent another tentacle down to join the other. He held Chase close, kissing his cheek and his lips as he pressed the second tentacle in, his breathing catching. "Ah… Elwood… yes…."

"Oh *fuck* yeah." Chase laughed giddily, groaning as his hole struggled to take on the added girth. Miraculously, there was no pain. He only felt a divine pleasure and the intense sensation of being filled.

It had been a long time since he'd been with someone, much longer than he dared to count. He'd expected some kind of physical resistance, perhaps a bit of discomfort, but there was none. Merrick fit inside of him as if they'd been molded for one another, and he couldn't believe how good it was.

Not even his wildest dreams could have ever compared to this.

Chase was fully bared, every inch of his body and soul given over in worship to the radiant god above him. The most exquisite sensation of all was feeling this deity tremble in his most intimate embrace, and it was both humbling and empowering.

Elwood Q. Chase, lowly ol' mortal magic enforcement detective, had Gordoth the Untouched giving up his title for a night in his bed.

The least he could do was let him know what a fine job he was doing.

"There you go, baby," Chase purred. "Give me all of that tentacle-dick… you feel so fuckin' good stretching' me out… fuck… no one's ever given it to me like you… I love you… fuck all, I love you so much. Come on, give it to me. I want you. I want all of you, baby…."

"Elwood." Merrick's voice cracked.

"Come on, baby," Chase urged. "Give it to me. Make me fuckin' come for you."

The next sound that came from Merrick's lips was a roar, so deep it vibrated the entire bed. He shifted, repositioning his body to pin Chase down, and he growled low, "Oh, and you will. Over… and over again."

As Merrick's hesitation faded, he thrust with more confidence. The two tentacles moved as one and plunged deep inside of Chase's body. He found a steady rhythm and pounded harder, a new energy taking over his once faltering movements.

"Ahhh, fuck!" Chase shouted, his knees trying to draw up against the new onslaught. He was getting close, so very close. Fuck, it was good, right on the edge of too much, it was—

Almost immediately, Merrick came to a full stop. "Am I hurting you?"

"No, no, no!" Chase shook his head. "Fuck, come on! Don't stop, baby boy! Please—*ahhh*, there we go!" He groaned low as Merrick got going again. "Come on! There!"

Merrick's back bowed as he thrust, and he growled hungrily. It didn't even sound human, a glimpse of the god hiding in this human shell. "Elwood... by all the gods...."

"I know, baby." Chase grunted, closing his eyes tight. "It's so good... fuck...." He tugged at the tentacles holding his arms down, freeing one hand so he could reach down and feel where Merrick was entering him. His rim was tender, wet, and now he couldn't stop touching himself.

He slid his fingers over the slippery tentacles thrusting away and let his head fall back against the bed. The sweet pressure of release was building up again, and he didn't want to lose it. He grabbed his cock with his other hand, quickly stroking himself back to hardness.

"No," Merrick suddenly snapped, several of his tentacles whipping Chase's hands back and pinning them to the sheets. "I shall give you your pleasure."

"Then fuckin' give it to me," Chase demanded, struggling against Merrick's tentacles. "Fuck! Please!"

Merrick's eyes raked over Chase's body, and his tentacles suddenly felt thicker. They were both pumping so hard and so fast and suddenly had focused in on that one spot—

"Ah, Merry!" Chase cried, his thighs trembling as he came. It hit him fast enough to make him gasp before taking a deep breath to power a strangled moan, his cock unloading all over his stomach and chest.

He was grateful for all of Merrick's tentacles keeping him firmly in place because he couldn't stop moving; his hips were slamming down to get more of that divine pressure as his thighs fought to close to stave off the impending overstimulation. His skin was on fire, and he felt like he was actually floating outside of his own body.

Each pulse from his cock was a hymn of pure ecstasy, sung with eager moans and breathless whispers, and just when Chase thought it was over, Merrick came.

Two fat loads flooded his hole, increasing the hot tension and sending him over the edge again. Chase was sobbing now, riding out every impossible quake as his cock shot across his stomach once more. His chest was too tight, and he was left wheezing as he struggled to come to terms with what had just happened.

It was impossible, beautiful, and he already wanted more.

"I love you," Merrick whispered before claiming Chase's lips, kissing him passionately. His tentacles had stopped moving but remained as they were, still seated inside of Chase's body.

"I love you," Chase mumbled, his voice weak. He was shaking, sweating, and miraculously it felt like he was still coming. The storm of sensation calmed when Merrick touched his cheek, and he could finally breathe again. "Heh. Definitely not the Untouched now."

Laughing, Merrick gave him another kiss. "I should think not." His tentacles relaxed, and he wiped the sweat from Chase's brow. "You are... amazing. This has been incredible."

"Me? Ha!" Chase grinned. "You're the one doin' all the work."

"Well, I am enjoying myself very much. I do not mind."

"Oh, trust me, Merry. I am not complainin'."

"I wish... I wish to turn you over now," Merrick confessed. "To... to hold you while I am inside you... I am sorry, I am having trouble describing what I want."

"It's okay." Chase stretched, waiting for Merrick to move off him before clumsily rolling over onto his side. "Mm, like this?"

"Yes," Merrick breathed, immediately pressing himself against Chase's back.

Chase shivered as Merrick stroked his belly, and he was startled by how emotional he suddenly felt. The touch was worshipful, and experiencing such affection for the part of his body he hated the most was making his eyes hot.

Merrick traced each and every stretch mark and scar, kissing Chase's shoulder as he gingerly withdrew his tentacles. "You are... so beautiful."

"So are you." Chase closed his eyes as he felt the nudge of another tentacle at his hole, and this one was different than the others. "Ah, bringing out the big guns, huh?"

"Are you using crude humor to mask your vulnerability?"

"Are you or are you not gonna fuck me with one of those giant tentacle-dicks?"

Merrick laughed and hugged Chase close. "Mm, well, that was my plan if you are still certain you want to have all of me."

"Come on," Chase urged. He didn't know how he wasn't passed out from exhaustion yet, but he wanted more. "I'm ready."

Merrick rubbed Chase's belly as he pushed inside, and he groaned. "Ah... Elwood...."

The stretch danced with pain, and Chase's eyes teared up. It was overwhelming enough to be held like this, but that massive tentacle-cock working him open was a whole new level. He'd never taken anything so big, and he almost wanted to laugh at how absurd it was.

It shouldn't fit. Fuck, there wasn't any way... but the ridges were going deeper and deeper until the knot was right there, pushing against his ass.

Merrick was taking his time, but Chase couldn't stop himself from crying out. Any threat of discomfort faded quickly, and Merrick didn't try to force his knot inside. He continued to kiss and pet Chase everywhere he could reach, his other tentacles wrapping all around him.

"Good, it feels so good," Chase managed to pant, his voice hitting a higher pitch when Merrick lifted his leg. It changed the angle, and the tentacle-dick seemed bigger, and the knot suddenly slipped in and made him moan.

Chase was lost to every fantastic thrust and the sounds of Merrick moaning in his ear, the tension in his body winding up for another orgasm. He could hardly believe it was happening, but he was too absorbed in the moment to question Merrick's divine bedroom prowess.

Despite having been a virgin for however many thousands of years, Merrick was impressive, not to mention a very fast learner. He seemed to be reading all of Chase's body language and dissecting all of his cries, trying to figure out what he liked the most.

He tilted Chase's body forward, nearly pushing him face-first down into the bed as he continued to pound into him.

"Oh, Merr," Chase groaned, rocking his body back to meet Merrick's thrusting. "God, yeah, just like this. Right there, right fuckin' there. Ah, baby boy, come on... gonna come. You're gonna make me fuckin' come!"

There, Chase was coming again. His skin was hot and tingling, and he ground down into the bed as his cock unloaded. Everything was sensitive and excited, and he was frantic to keep the feeling going for as long as he could.

"I love you," Merrick gasped, his strong grip trembling as he redoubled his efforts and pounded Chase's body even harder. "Ah, Elwood, I love you so much!"

"I love you too. Fuck, I love you. I love you!" Chase screamed when Merrick came, the knot swelling inside of him and creating so much intense pressure that he climaxed immediately. It was like going mad, trying to grapple with so much at once, and he sobbed loudly, pivoting his body between humping the bed and slamming back on Merrick's tentacle-dick.

The pleasure went on for several minutes, the two of them locked together as they both quivered and shook. Chase couldn't seem to catch his breath, and it still felt like he was coming. The bliss finally faded, and he went limp, utterly exhausted.

His hole was still clenching around Merrick's tentacle-dick, and the slightest shift made them groan in unison. He weakly reached for Merrick's hand, drawing it up to rest against his chest.

"Well," Merrick said, noticeably out of breath, "I think that I may need a moment before we continue."

"Ah, did I manage to wear out a god?" Chase teased, enjoying how Merrick's tentacles coiled all around him. "Go me."

"It is very overwhelming," Merrick replied after a thoughtful moment. "The physical pleasure aside, knowing I am sharing myself with you... that we are being joined... it is...." He paused again, visibly fighting to find the right words. "It is like our souls are touching."

"Yeah." Chase smiled at that, and he turned to kiss Merrick's cheek. "It's pretty damn awesome, huh?"

"I am very glad you were my first." Merrick ducked his head against Chase's shoulder. "I would not have wanted this any other way."

"Even with the whole world-might-be-ending bit?"

Merrick snorted. "That I could do without. But as we have already established, they lack the key ingredient to conduct the ritual successfully."

"Somebody with stars in their blood, yeah?"

"Exactly so."

Chase stretched his legs, listening to his hips and his knees pop. "Mmm. Damn."

"Are you all right?" Merrick's brow furrowed. "I can heal you if you—"

"No, no, I'm okay." Chase grinned. "Oh, I am so okay. Just old, Merr." He rolled his eyes at Merrick's flat stare. "Yes, I know you're technically thousands of years older than me, but arthritis isn't exactly a godly problem, is it?"

"Fair point." Merrick gently pulled his tentacle-dick out from between Chase's legs.

"Fuck." Chase loved how Merrick's impressive come leaking out of him felt, and he had to touch himself. He gasped when he found his hole so open and wet, slipping his fingers inside to feel how loose he was.

Merrick's hand joined his, tentatively tracing around the edge of Chase's hole. "Elwood... you feel so different... I want...." His eyes were wide and black as he looked at Chase, pleading, "I want to see."

"Help yourself, baby boy." Chase had to hold back a laugh at how quickly Merrick wiggled down between his legs. A few tentacles abruptly turned him flat on his back and spread his legs. "Ah, mmm, eager, are we?"

"Yes." Merrick stroked the underside of Chase's thighs, one of his smaller tentacles slipping inside Chase's wet hole to explore.

"Mmm...." Chase dropped his head back as the tentacle twisted at an impossible angle, and his cock twitched. He could feel himself trying to get hard again, and he reached down to stroke his fingers over the top of Merrick's short hair.

"You are so soft," Merrick whispered in awe. "I did this to you…?"

"Yeah, you did." Chase chuckled. "You're welcome to do it any damn time you'd like."

"I am afraid I would not accomplish much if I took you based on my desire, seeing as how I want you incessantly."

"Mm, I wouldn't complain." Chase gasped as the tentacle pushed deep enough to make his toes curl. Yup, definitely hard again. His arousal was rekindled, and he moaned as the tentacle curled upward to press against his prostate.

"I wish to be inside of you again," Merrick said quietly, the slim tentacle rocking steadily. "May I have you again, Elwood?"

"Fuck yeah." Chase dragged Merrick up against his chest to kiss him, wrapping his legs around his hips. He felt the second tentacle-dick, the other big monster, pressing against his hole. "Mmm, yes, come on, give it to me."

Merrick took his time, pushing in inch by inch until the tentacle-dick was thrusting alongside the smaller tentacle still pumping inside of Chase's ass. His knot popped in and swelled, and he growled in absolute delight. "Elwood… by all the gods…!"

Chase gave himself over to Merrick's every thrust, marveling at the incredible feeling of both tentacles fucking him so efficiently. They moved together as one massive girth, occasionally parting so the smaller one could push against the sweet spot inside of him while the other kept on slamming.

Merrick used his other tentacles to lift Chase's hips from the bed, apparently seeking the angle that would make him scream the loudest. Even in the midst of such primal passion, Merrick was touching Chase all over, stroking his thighs and the curve of his stomach.

"I love you, I love you, fuck, I love you," Chase chanted, clinging to Merrick's forearms. His body felt like it was floating, the relentless pounding taking him over the edge of climax so many times, he lost count. It was an endless wave of bliss, riding the crest of one orgasm right into the next.

Even when Merrick came with a joyous roar, he kept stroking Chase's intimate parts to coax one final climax from him.

Chase was trembling, and his eyes were stinging with tears. His entire body was heavy, hot, and he could barely lift his head. He didn't know what to say, and he kissed Merrick, putting everything he had into it with the hope that the message was received—that he still couldn't believe this had happened, the man he loved was a god and loved him too.

He was absolutely exhausted, sore, and more than a little sticky. Fuckin' worth it.

"I love you," Merrick said, bringing the covers over them and snuggling against Chase's side.

"Love you too." Chase lifted his arm so Merrick could cuddle closer, and they stayed like that for several long moments, quiet and happy.

Merrick tidied them both up with a thought, and Chase was grateful he didn't have to get up and grab a shower. He really didn't want to move. Maybe ever.

"I am very happy," Merrick said, his eyes dark and full of stars when he looked up at Chase. "Thank you."

"Ha, thank *you*. I'm happy too. Really fucking happy." Chase beamed. "So, how does it feel to finally be Touched?"

"Wonderful," Merrick replied with a bright smile.

"Yeah?"

"Now I understand what all the fuss was about at those orgies."

Chase cackled. "Dammit, I love you."

"And I love you." Merrick kissed Chase's cheek. "So very much."

"I love you so much it's downright *squidiculous*."

"Was that…." Merrick snorted. "Did you just…?"

"Make an amazing pun? I *conch* believe you have to ask."

Merrick laughed. "Oh, that is even worse!"

"Come on. We both know what a *sucker* you are for 'em." Chase was delighted by the way Merrick was laughing now, and he had to keep going. "Seeing as how you're currently *octopying* my bed, I wanna make sure you stay for a while."

"Ah, and you think this is working?"

"I know it is. Out of all the places in the whole wide *tunaverse*, this is exactly where you want to be."

"Tunaverse?" Merrick was laughing even harder. "Come on!"

"Hey! You try coming up with these damn jokes instead of just laughin' at them!" Chase laughed until he was cut off by a yawn he tried to hide with his palm.

"Mmm, I suppose I have worn you out finally?" Merrick petted his hair.

"I'll be ready to go in no time."

"Bedtime now," Merrick ordered with a smirk. "We still have much work to do tomorrow."

"Meh. Work is overrated."

"Sleep."

"I love you."

"And I love you."

"Really?" Chase teased, laying his head down and getting comfortable. "Like *really*, really love me?"

"I love you so much… it is quite *squidiculous*."

Chase laughed. "See? That one is great."

"Sleep sweetly, my mate," Merrick whispered, kissing Chase's brow as his tentacles squeezed him all over.

"Mmm, good night, baby boy." Chase melted into the wonderful embrace and closed his eyes. Here in Merrick's many arms, he was safe, loved, and utterly content.

It was like coming home.

Sleep came quickly for Chase, and he slept long and hard. He dreamed about floating castles up in the stars and strange green winds. He didn't wake up until he heard his phone beeping, and he reached over to swat off the alarm. That's when he noticed he had a new notification.

It was a text message alert.

He was still wrapped up in Merrick's tentacles, and he wiggled around trying to free himself. He didn't know why, but he had the weirdest feeling he needed to read the message.

"Good morning," Merrick said, his tentacles drawing Chase back in so he could kiss him. He'd clearly been awake for some time. "Mm. It is very early. Did you sleep well, my love?"

"Fuckin' amazing. Mmm." Chase took a moment to enjoy how handsome Merrick looked in his bed, his face almost glowing in the first hint of morning light. He could imagine waking up like this every morning. "Damn."

"What?" Merrick blinked.

"Just you, baby boy," Chase replied, kissing him sweetly. He heard his phone beep again. "Mm, hang on one sec."

"Here." Merrick's tentacles reached over to the bedside table and came back with Chase's phone. "I heard it make a sound, but I did not want to pry."

"Thanks." Chase tapped on the screen to access his messages. "It's not a big deal. Hell, if it was dispatch, they just woulda called."

The text was from Ollie, and it had been sent around one in the morning. Reading it made Chase's heart drop down into his gut.

heyyy sorry to bug u so but im a lik srunk ans i think i know where those cultist dudes are. call me. cuz its like in my parking lot.

Immediately, Chase dialed him.

"What is wrong?" Merrick asked, frowning at the distressed look on Chase's face.

"It's Ollie." The call kept ringing. "He said he mighta figured out where the cultists are. He said they were in his fucking parking lot, and now he's not picking up."

"Perhaps he had a long night?" Merrick made a face. "His alcohol consumption is concerning."

"Yeah, I know, but this doesn't feel right." Chase frowned when the call went to voicemail. He tried to call again, getting out of bed and looking for his clothes.

Merrick was up behind him, all of his tentacles vanishing in a quick whirl. "We can drive over there if you wish."

"No, we need to get there like, like, right now." Chase fumbled for some underwear from a pile of what was hopefully clean laundry. His heart felt fluttery and weird, and he could not shake the feeling that something was terribly wrong.

"Here." Merrick touched Chase's shoulder.

In a quick flash, they were both dressed. Chase was wearing a suit from his closet and his trusty hat, and Merrick had put on the same suit he'd wore yesterday.

"Okay. Let's go," Chase said, still frantically dialing Ollie's phone in hopes of an answer. "You gotta take us there now. Like, wiggle your god tentacles and poof!"

"Elwood," Merrick warned, "I cannot do that. I will not be able to explain how we got there if—"

"Right now, fuckin' please! For the fuckin' love of all the gods, Merr!" Chase pleaded, grabbing Merrick's arm. "I can't fucking explain it, but I know something is fucked-up. I can't wait. Can you please just do this for me? Please?"

Merrick frowned, but he nodded in agreement. "Yes, Elwood. We will go." He laid his hand over Chase's, and in a blink, they were inside Ollie's apartment.

As soon as Chase looked around, he thought he was going to throw up.

The entire apartment had been torn apart; the chair was knocked over, liquor bottles were scattered across the floor, and there was a small splatter of blood on the wall by the remnants of the shattered door.

Ollie was gone.

Chapter 13.

"Don't worry," Milo was saying. "We're gonna find him."

Chase nodded wearily from his spot on Ollie's couch, cradling his head in his hands.

This was a nightmare.

Merrick had returned to Chase's apartment to get his car, and Chase stayed behind to call it in as a kidnapping. He refused to accept any minimum-waiting-period bullshit. Someone had taken his nephew, and he had an excellent idea of who.

Ol' Jeff and his cultist buddies needed someone with stars in their blood, and now they had one.

The question nagging at the back of his mind was how did they know?

Ollie never registered his ability, so there wouldn't be any record of it. There was always a chance someone at the department or another client had figured it out, but so far they weren't finding a connection to any of the known cultists.

Calling Ollie's parents was awful, especially when Chase couldn't tell them much other than the investigation was ongoing. He swore he would do everything in his power to bring Ollie home safely, wishing he could tell them more.

Then again, maybe it was better they didn't know their son had been taken by insane cultists who were going to sacrifice him to perform a ritual to end the world by waking up some crazy ol' god.

Fuck.

Watching his fellow officers and Milo crowd into the little apartment didn't bring Chase much comfort. There were dozens more out in the city searching too. He appreciated all the effort, but he had a god as his partner, and they still hadn't been able to find these assholes.

"Do you need anything?" Merrick asked quietly, hovering next to him.

"A stiff drink. Like, ten of them." Chase rubbed his temples. "We get the all-clear to go talk to Daisy?"

"No."

"Why the fuck not?" Chase demanded angrily. "We know she's hiding something! She's gotta be! The truth spell—"

"It was cast without consent." Merrick shook his head. "She has already been instructed not to speak to anyone except internal affairs. We could be charged with interfering with IA's case if we try to talk to her again."

"Well, what the fuck do we do now?" Chase wished he had a cigarette. "There's nothing fucking here. We already know that."

"I am sorry."

Merrick had taken the liberty of using his full godly powers to search the apartment for clues and found nothing that would help lead them to Ollie. Of course they couldn't tell anyone that, so they had to let the mortal search continue.

"We've gotta find him," Chase said firmly, trying not to give in to despair. "If anything happens to him, I'm gonna go fuckin' nuts."

"We will find him," Merrick insisted.

"Look, we see them coming in on the parking lot security camera, but they never left. So we know they took him right smack outta here, which means a portal, right?" Milo dropped his voice. "I can't be, like, totally sure, but I have a theory about why we can't find these guys."

"And that is?"

"So Loch is always taking Sloane to all these magical worlds with, like, porno temples and stuff," Milo explained, glancing around to make sure no one else was close enough to overhear. "What if the cultist dudes are hanging out in one of those places?"

"The what now?" Chase's head hurt.

"There are hidden places created by the gods between this world and the next," Merrick whispered hurriedly. "We once used them for worship and celebration, but they have been lost to mortals for centuries. They are impossible to access unless a god has shared the spell, and every location is unique."

"Sloane and Loch got married in one of these places," Milo said. "They're still out there, and Jeffy boy sure did have some weird old-ass artifacts, like that silencing totem."

"You think he found a spell to take him to one of these other-world places?" Chase asked.

"Would explain why we can't find them."

"Can't you go to these places and look around?" Chase asked Merrick hopefully.

"There are hundreds of them, perhaps even thousands." Merrick sighed. "It would take too long to search them individually, and not even I know all of their locations. Some gods kept very private worlds."

"Like the porn temple," Milo chimed in.

"Exactly so."

Chase picked up some of the papers scattered haphazardly across the coffee table. Every page was filled with long lines of scribbled notes in Ollie's handwriting. He hadn't given them much of a look before, but a familiar street name now caught his eye.

It was then he realized the pages were a list of sentences starting with "The cultist dillweeds are on" and then a different street name was plugged in.

Ollie had been trying to narrow down the cultists' location for them. He'd been writing all the city's street names, going block by block and crossing them all out until he wrote his own street down.

The last few sentences were also uncrossed, and reading them made Chase's stomach churn.

The cultist dillweeds are on Hold Street.
The cultists are here at the apartments.
Parking lot.
My building.
The cultists are here.

Having been reading over his shoulder, Merrick murmured, "He was trying to help us."

"Here, let me, uh, inventory those," Milo said, taking the papers from Chase. "Don't need any nosy people wondering what Ollie was trying to do here."

"Wait, there's something on the back," Chase said.

Milo flipped it over. "As the words speak, the deed must be done, but only when the Faedra's wings flutter and the Vulgora bask in the sun."

"What the fuck does that mean?" Chase demanded.

"It's a time," Merrick said quickly. "Ollie must have been able to translate more of the ritual."

"Well, what the fuck does Faedra's wings flutterin' and that Vulgoofus shit mean?"

"Eh, give or take...." Merrick grimaced. "Six o'clock."

"Fuck."

The three of them had agreed they would say Ollie had been taken for his translation skills, not because of his starsight. It was a small thing, but Chase was determined to keep Ollie's gift a secret like he'd promised.

It was the least he could do, though a little voice in the back of his mind reminded him that keeping Ollie's secret was pointless if he was dead.

"Thanks, Milo." Chase frowned. "So what the fuck do we do now?"

"Sloane and Loch are searching the city for any signs of portals and other suspicious witch stuff. I know you guys did your thing here, but I'm gonna keep looking too." Milo offered a reassuring smile. "We're gonna figure this out, okay?"

"Are you insinuating I missed something, Mr. Evans?" Merrick narrowed his eyes.

"No, I'm just saying that a second look can't hurt, okay?" Milo held up his hands. "Calm down, Your Royal Tentacleness."

"That nickname is highly inappropriate."

"Well, we're not gonna get any shit done here sittin' on our asses." Chase stood abruptly, looking to Merrick. "You still got all those case files, right?"

"Yes."

"Let's go."

Back to Chase's apartment they went, and Merrick brought the files in with them. Chase pulled everything out and spread the papers on the dining room table. When he ran out of room there, he continued over on the coffee table and then the floor.

He didn't have super godly powers like Loch or Merrick, and he didn't have magical starlight like Sloane. Hell, he didn't even have the forensic or technical skills like Milo and Daisy. He was a painfully average mortal in many respects, and going back through these case files and hoping he'd find something was all he could do.

It made him feel helpless, and he couldn't stop thinking about Ollie. He wished they had never come to him for the damn translation. Logically, he knew he wasn't responsible, but that didn't stop him from feeling like shit anyway.

Especially as the clock kept ticking away.

"There has to be something we're missing," Chase kept telling himself. "People just don't fuckin' vanish, porn temple or no fuckin' porn temple."

Merrick didn't say much, choosing to focus on the files and use his godly powers to tirelessly speed-read through them. He chased down the tiniest inconsistency, made countless phone calls, but still found nothing that would help them.

They hadn't heard anything from Sloane and Loch yet, and Milo had only texted them to tell them he had found absolutely squat but was still searching.

It was half past four o'clock in the afternoon when Chase finally snapped. He'd been reading for so long his eyes hurt, and he went right for the whiskey. He trudged back to the sofa to pour a glass, glancing over at Merrick expectantly.

"What?"

"Waiting for you to tell me not to drink on the clock."

"I think, considering the circumstances, I am willing to make an exception," Merrick said, offering a gentle smile. "At least this one time."

"Thanks." Chase tipped the glass back.

"May I offer you physical comfort?"

"You ain't gotta ask." Chase smiled and patted the cushion next to him. "Come on over, Merry."

Merrick sat down and took Chase's hand. He snuggled against his side, resting his head on his shoulder. "I believe we will be triumphant and rescue Ollie."

"Yeah?" Chase resisted the urge to scoff. "Even with the odds stacked against us like this?"

"I did not think I would find a mate of my own, and yet, here we are. I've replayed our evening of making love together countless times, and I cannot imagine it being more perfect." Merrick looked up at Chase, his jaw set stubbornly. "I had given up hope before. I will not give up now."

"Countless times, huh?"

"Of course that is what you focused on." Merrick rolled his eyes.

"No, no, I hear you. Keep the faith, have hope, but I'm definitely intrigued by this 'countless times' business."

"You are revolting."

"I know." Chase sighed, laughing mirthlessly. "Sorry. Was trying to lighten the mood. It's not working."

"I am very sorry." Merrick petted Chase's beard. "Would this be an appropriate time to kiss you?"

"Knock yourself out." Chase bowed his head to meet Merrick halfway, enjoying a sweet and reassuring kiss. "Mm, thank you. I needed that."

"Happy to help." Merrick smiled. "Just as I am sure we will have infinite bouts of lovemaking, I am certain that we will find him."

Chase wanted to believe him, but it was hard with less than two hours to go. They needed a miracle. He laid his hand over Merrick's on his cheek, trying to be brave. "Thank you, Merr." He smirked wearily as Merrick continued to play with his beard. "You like this rug on my face, huh?"

"Yes. I enjoy touching your beard."

"Yeah?" Chase chuckled. "Running your fingers through it?"

"It is a very nice beard," Merrick insisted. "I like it."

He had the nicest beard. I always used to tell him that I couldn't wait to run my fingers through it again.

Chase knew he'd heard someone say that before, but who....

"Wait, wait." Chase jumped up from the couch, hurrying back over to the dining table where Slappy's file was. He flipped through and pulled out all the mugshot photos.

In the pictures from Slappy's arrest, he was clean-shaven. He'd also been clean-shaven in the photograph Chase had seen in his office.

"Son of a bitch."

"What is it?" Merrick asked, joining him at the table. "Do you have something?"

"Daisy talked about wanting to get all creepy and rub up on Slappy's beard, right?"

"I vaguely recall something to that effect. Why?"

"Look at the pictures," Chase hissed. "When he got popped for fraud, no beard. The photograph that he had hung in his office posing with the Lord Collins painting? No fuckin' beard."

"I am not following."

"Daisy told us she hadn't seen him since the last time she visited him in prison." Chase shook the file. "So how did she know he has a beard now?"

"She lied," Merrick hissed.

"She had to have seen him *recently* to know he'd grown that big ol' sexy beard!"

"You believe she participated in his murder?"

"Maybe she was the one who tried to make him give up the painting. Who knows!" Chase threw up his hands. "But she sure as fuck lied about when she saw him last."

"How did she beat the truth spell?"

"I don't know." Chase was already putting on his coat and fumbling for his hat. "We gotta go. She fuckin' knows something. I don't care if you have to slap her with all of your fuckin' tentacles, we are gonna make her talk."

"You suspect a deeper involvement with the cult?"

"I fuckin' suspect she's our only lead right now," Chase said. "We've got fuck all nothing. We have to try. I don't care we're not supposed to go talk to her. Fuck the stupid goddamn internal investigation!" His voice cracked. "If anything happens to Ollie... I...."

"We're going. Now." Merrick reached out and grabbed Chase's hand. "Hold on tightly."

The room suddenly spun and disappeared, and Chase found himself standing outside of Daisy's house. He was a little dizzy, and he leaned against Merrick to steady himself. "Fuck, that's still weird."

"I apologize," Merrick said, holding on to Chase's arm to help him over to Daisy's front door.

"Totally forgiven." Chase banged away at the door with his fist and did not stop until it opened.

"Chase? Merrick?" Daisy pouted when she saw the two of them, only opening the door a few inches. "You're not supposed to be here. My representative said—"

"Fuck your representative," Chase snapped. "My fucking nephew is missing, and we know you lied to us." He pushed his way forward into the house, swinging the door wide open and forcing Daisy to frantically backpedal.

"Hey, hey! Just take it easy!" Daisy held up her hands, nearly tripping over the coffee table. "Can you please calm down?"

"Your little fucking buddies took my nephew for your stupid fucking ritual!" Chase barked. "Start talking. Now!"

"Your nephew?" Daisy's eyes widened, and she suddenly smiled. "No way."

"Fucking excuse me?" Chase slammed the door shut once Merrick was inside, and he stalked back toward her. "If you know something, I fuckin' swear—"

"If they've got him, it's over." Daisy laughed hysterically, clapping and dancing in place. "It's all over! It's almost time! It's too late for you!"

"No," Chase whispered, his heart clenching up tight and his mind reeling from Daisy's shocking display. "It can't be!"

"It's too late for all of you!" Daisy continued to cheer. "Ha! It's already after five o'clock! Look! It's five ten! Fifty minutes to go! Salgumel is finally going to awaken and bring all the gods with him!"

"Not all of them," Merrick hissed furiously, stepping in front of Chase and advancing on Daisy. He held out his hand, several tentacles unfurling from his sleeve and coiling around her neck and shoulders, forcing her to kneel. "Feel my divine flesh and look upon my true face, mortal!"

"No!" Daisy screamed in horror, gasping and clawing at Merrick's tight grip. "It can't... it just can't be!"

Merrick's eyes were glowing almost white, and he roared, "I am Gordoth, brother of Salgumel, Shartorath, Yeris, Ulgon, Elgrirath, Zarnorach, Xarbon, Solmach, Eb, Ebb, Ebbeth, and Lozathin. I was spawned by Baub, the child of Zunnerath and Halandrach, they who were born of Etheril and Xarapharos, descended directly from Great Azaethoth himself!"

Daisy cried, clinging to Gordoth's tentacles and sobbing, "I'm so sorry! I didn't know! I didn't know it was you!"

"Speak the truth now or suffer my wrath," Merrick snarled, his eyes black now as he stared Daisy down. "How did you know about Oleander's gift?"

Chase sucked in a sharp breath and licked his lips. Watching Merrick go full-on angry god was kind of hot—*shit*.

No, revisit that thought later. Now was not the time.

"At Slappy's house!" Daisy cried. "Milo was on the phone with me while you guys were there. I heard him asking about the guy doing your translating and figured out it was your nephew. He worked for the department, and I looked up his address."

"Fuck," Chase hissed.

"How did you withhold the truth from us when we questioned you before?" Merrick demanded.

"I knew you guys were gonna come here." Daisy closed her eyes, swallowing down a whimper and taking a deep breath. "I knew what you would ask me, so I knew what to say. Like how I really didn't want Slappy to get hurt because I wanted him to *die* after what he did. It was bad enough that he broke my heart, but then he went and turned his back on the coven.

"I tried reasoning with him when we found out he had one of the Lord Collins paintings, but he refused! He wouldn't even sell it to us because he knew we'd be desperate enough to steal it, and he'd have a chance to make money off the insurance claim like he did before. He cared more about money than anything else, even the gods!"

"The cult," Chase realized out loud. "You're the one running the fuckin' show. That's how you got around those other questions!

Makin' us think Jeff was trying to keep you away for your own good, but he was trying to snatch up your spot!"

"I was," Daisy confessed. "At least, well, of this chapter. But I really did dump Jeff. I dumped him because he pushed me out. He turned everyone in the coven against me once they knew you guys were gonna be questioning me. He said I couldn't be trusted, even though that bastard knew I wouldn't say anything. Not when we were so close to waking up Salgumel!"

"Right, yeah, that's just terrible," Chase drawled, raising his voice to snap, "Now tell me where my fuckin' nephew is! Do you guys have him stashed in one of those stupid god worlds? Huh? Where is he?"

"I can't... I can't tell you!" Daisy's eyes widened. "It wouldn't matter anyway! The ritual is almost ready! There's nothing you can do—ulgh!"

Merrick's grip tightened around Daisy's neck. "Speak, mortal!"

"The orchard," she whimpered helplessly, tears streaming down her face. "They've gone to Babbeth's orchard!"

"Thank you." Merrick bopped her on the forehead with one of the tentacles, and she crumpled to the floor.

She didn't move.

"What the hell did you do?" Chase blinked in shock.

"Exactly what I yelled at my nephew for doing to you," Merrick replied, looking almost sheepish. "I erased her memory. She will wake up with no recollection of what has happened."

"And the risk of her remembering?"

"Worth taking to save Ollie," Merrick confirmed. He closed his eyes briefly. "I have told Azzath where we are headed. They will join us as soon as they can. Are you ready?"

"I'm ready," Chase said. He grabbed Merrick in a tight hug, pressing a quick kiss to his lips. "Let's go."

"We have no idea what's waiting for us," Merrick said. "I must take on my true form so I can fully access my power." His brow wrinkled up in that endearing way Chase knew well. "Please do not be alarmed."

"I already told you," Chase said firmly, "I don't care. I'll love you, bat wings and all, and I'll still want you to fuck me stupid every day for the rest of our lives."

"Although crude, that is very kind."

"Right?"

"Hang on."

The world around them vanished, and Chase was struck by another wave of vertigo. He closed his eyes, waiting for it to pass. His feet left solid ground for a few seconds, and Merrick's arms were gone. They were replaced by strong tentacles, and Chase held on tightly.

"We are here," Merrick whispered.

It was still his voice, but it was deeper, rumbling, and somehow inside Chase's head and his ears at the same time.

Chase looked around to see they were standing in an orchard, an endless field of black trees with strange shriveled fruit hanging from the highest branches. The sky was dark, as if a bad storm was on the way. The air smelled slightly sour, and it was clouded with a faint veil of smoke.

Chase looked over to Merrick and tried not to gasp.

Merrick was a *dragon*.

He was as big as a house, with black-and-gold scales and massive horns spiraling out of his head. His eyes were empty black pits, and there was a long beard of tentacles at his chin. He had powerful front arms with large talons, but his lower body was a mass of giant tentacles like an octopus.

These were the thick coils holding Chase up, and he held on a little tighter, completely awestruck.

Merrick's wings were indeed like a bat's, grand and glittering even in the low light of this world. The webbing was so thin that it was almost translucent, like whispers of golden cobwebs stretched between each skeletal finger.

This was Gordoth, the god himself in the flesh, and Chase momentarily lost himself in his incredible visage. His mouth was open, but he couldn't speak.

"Are you all right?" Merrick asked, bowing his head down. "Am I that… frightening…?"

He was the one who sounded afraid, and Chase wanted to laugh.

"As if I could ever be scared of you." Chase smiled, reaching out to touch Merrick's snout. He stroked the slick scales and the coils of his tentacle beard, kissing his nose. "No matter what you are, you're mine."

Merrick made a grumbling sound, perhaps a purr, and he leaned into Chase's hands. "My mate."

"My mate," Chase confirmed. He took a deep breath, looking around the creepy trees. "We ready?"

"Yes." Merrick lifted Chase up, urging him onto his back. "Hold on. We must hurry. The orchard is vast and will take some time to search."

"We got, like, forty minutes." Chase straddled Merrick's neck above his wings, hugging him tightly. He closed his eyes and hissed, "Is this a bad time to tell you I don't like heights?"

"Do not worry. We are not flying." Merrick lowered his head and tucked his arms back at an awkward angle next to his wings.

"We're not?"

"No." Merrick lunged forward, propelled by the tentacles that made up his tail, slithering at an incredible speed through the trees. "I do not want them to see us coming."

Chase nearly fell off and wrapped his legs around Merrick's neck, cursing loudly as he tried desperately to hold on. "Fuck, fuck, fuck!"

Merrick's mass was so great that the trees were crushed beneath his belly as he tore through them, but it didn't make the slightest sound. The giant god moved silently except for the wind whipping all around them as he slithered away.

Chase clenched his teeth and ducked his head, hanging on to his hat and praying to any gods who might be listening—this one included—that they would find Ollie safe and alive.

They were almost out of time.

"There!" Merrick bellowed.

Ahead, there was a small clearing in the trees. There was a large fire and twenty or more people in dark robes surrounding an altar.

There! It was Ollie!

Ollie was lying on the altar, unmoving, and his shirt was ripped open. Jeff was standing beside him, leading a frantic chant and wielding a giant knife.

As Merrick burst through the trees, the robed cultists immediately screamed and started to scatter. Someone tripped over the firepit, sending embers scattering and catching the dried grass, creating an immediate brush fire that rapidly spread.

"Release that mortal at once!" Merrick roared, rising up on his tail of tentacles to tower over the flaming chaos, snarling furiously. "If you dare harm him, you shall know my wrath!"

Jeff hadn't budged from his place at the altar even as his eyes bulged in terror. Instead of taking this chance to flee, however, he turned to the altar with the dagger raised high above his head.

"No!" Chase screamed, throwing himself off Merrick and stumbling to his feet. The fire was burning him and his hat had flown off, but he didn't care. Faster, he had to move faster; he had to stop him—

The blade sunk right into Ollie's chest.

CHAPTER 14.

OLLIE SCREAMED, wide-awake from whatever spell was holding him down. Blood gushed out from the wound as he grabbed at the dagger.

Jeff kept pushing and pushing, shouting, "Rise, Salgumel! Come! Rain nightmares upon my enemies! Rise, now!"

Chase bolted toward the altar, but his legs felt like they were in water. He couldn't move fast enough; he was just too damn slow. Anguish tore at his heart and refused to let go of it, his mind overcome by fury and rage and torn apart right down to his core. "Ollie! No! No!"

Merrick was faster, his long tail swinging outward and knocking Jeff several yards away into the trees.

His body made a distinct *thunk* as it struck the ground.

Chase threw himself at the altar, reaching for Ollie's hands. "Ollie! God, no!" He tried pressing his hands over the wound, cutting himself on the exposed blade. "Shit! Just hold on! Hang on!"

"Unc...?" Ollie stared up at Chase in total disbelief, his eyes dull and sluggish. He coughed, blood spraying out over his lips, and his head fell back with a groan.

"Hey, hey," Chase pleaded, wishing he wasn't so fuck awful with healing magic. He couldn't think of the simplest spell, and he was watching Ollie die right in front of him. "It's me. Okay, kiddo? It's me, I'm here. Wake up, okay? I need you to wake up!"

"Let me," Merrick said, rushing over to join them, his tail tentacles curling around the dagger and gently urging Chase to back away. The ends of his tentacles began to glow.

"Please…. Merry…." Chase stumbled out of the way, a sob breaking free when he saw Ollie's eyes close completely. He looked down at his hands, soaked in his blood and Ollie's, and his grief turned into a blinding rage.

It was over. Ollie was dying, and the ritual would be complete.

And there was nothing he could do.

"Ughhh…." From behind them, Jeff had recovered and was stumbling to his feet. There was no sign of the other cultists.

Chase didn't know what had happened to them, and he didn't care. He had spent this entire case feeling useless and weak, and he was sick of it. He was too weak to save the world, much less his own nephew.

Something inside of him *snapped*.

"Any moment now," Jeff declared triumphantly, laughing. "Our Lord Salgumel will descend onto Aeon. You're too late. You're all too—"

Chase took his gun from his holster and shot Jeff in the knee.

"What the fuck!" Jeff roared in pain, dropping down and holding his leg. "You shot me!"

"Yeah, and I might do it again," Chase snarled, stalking toward him. "Just had to make sure you didn't try to wiggle away through a portal."

"I'm warded!" Jeff screamed furiously. "You can't hurt me!"

"Ancient wards are great for magic," Chase agreed, his hands trembling as he reholstered his gun. "But against modern ballistics? Not so much. Be sure to complain to your buddy Salgumel all about it."

"That's… stupid! You're stupid!"

"Says the guy bleeding." Chase grabbed Jeff by his collar, hefting him up to his feet and slamming him up against a tree. He reared back and slammed his fist into the side of Jeff's face.

Jeff grunted, his arms flailing outward and trying to fight back.

Chase barely felt Jeff's fists, so consumed in his anger that all he could focus on was the pain brewing inside of him. He started punching Jeff, over and over, becoming more unhinged with every blow.

"See?" he spat. "I can't set you on fire, I can't burn you up, but I can sure as fuck break your face!" He grabbed the sides of Jeff's head, bashing his forehead right into his nose. He watched Jeff collapse, hissing, "Ain't magic a bitch."

The bandage had fallen off Jeff's face, and the rotten handprint was bared. Chase could see Jeff's teeth gleaming through the hole, and he lifted his leg, driving the heel of his shoe right down into it.

Howling in pain, Jeff tried to roll away, but Chase wouldn't let him.

He kept kicking, screaming over Jeff as he shouted, "You piece of fucking shit! Fuck you! Fuck your god! Fuck your stupid rotten fuckin' face—"

"Hey! Chase!" Someone grabbed his arm.

Chase instinctively jerked back, turning to find Sloane behind him. "Sloane!"

"Hey, hey, take it easy," Sloane soothed, urging Chase away from Jeff. "He's done, okay? He's not going anywhere. It's over."

Chase shuddered and looked down at his bloody hands. He couldn't tell whose was what now, and his knuckles were raw. "Ollie... I...."

"It's gonna be okay." Sloane firmly squeezed Chase's shoulder.

"But Ollie...?" Tears ran down Chase's cheeks and into his beard as he looked past Sloane to the altar.

Merrick was still there, his tentacles curled around Ollie tight. There was another beast here now, a dragon like Merrick but taller and leaner. It had powerful hind legs, a long neck, and an even longer tentacled tail. Its wings were easily twice as big as Merrick's and shimmered like diamonds.

Loch. No.... Azaethoth.

His tentacles had joined Merrick's, and Ollie's body was glowing with a blinding light. It was all the colors of the rainbow and somehow none at all, so bright that it hurt Chase to look at.

"What are they doing?" Chase demanded.

"Saving him," Sloane said. "Come on." He urged Chase to follow him.

"But it's too late, isn't it?" Chase wiped his face hurriedly. "The ritual, they got his blood...."

"Have faith, mortal," Loch said, turning his giant head toward Chase. "The ritual has failed."

"What?"

"It is his heart," Merrick replied. "Though stars run brightly in his blood, Oleander's heart is not whole."

"The resurrection." Chase took Ollie's hand, frowning at how cold it felt. "He gave a piece of himself to his old boyfriend."

"His heart is broken and not a sufficient source of power for this ritual." Merrick bowed his head down to nuzzle Chase's shoulder. "Salgumel will not wake tonight, but…."

"But?" Chase stared into Merrick's empty eye sockets and over to Loch's dark depths.

"I don't know what more I can do for him," Merrick said quietly. "His soul is already trying to break away from his body."

Chase felt the start of a scream climbing its way out of his throat. "No," he grunted, struggling to keep it down. "No fuckin' way." He pushed Merrick, barking, "What kind of gods are you guys, huh? You can't save one fuckin' person?"

"Elwood, please—"

"No!" Chase threw himself on top of Ollie, shoving all the tentacles out of his way. "No, no, no!" He could see the gash left behind by the dagger, and it wasn't bleeding anymore.

It wasn't bleeding because….

"No," he whimpered, touching Ollie's hair and face. Fuck, he was already getting so cold. "Do something. Please. Anything! Come on!"

"We cannot," Merrick said, hanging his head low. "Bringing someone back from the dead is beyond our power."

"Useless-ass immortal fuckin' shitheads!" Chase roared. "Come the fuck on! Can't you wave your little tentacles around and fuckin' do something? Make some fuckin' sparkles of starlight?"

"Elwood!" Merrick suddenly snapped. "Your lighter!"

"My what?" Chase stared. "What are you talking about?"

"The fire spell you use to light your cigarette! *Ignis vitae*!"

"I don't… I don't understand!"

"Oleander has not been dead very long!" Merrick urged. "We may be able to bring his soul back to his body before it tries to leave this world! Please, trust me!"

Chase didn't hesitate. He trusted Merrick completely, and he stretched his hand above his head, snapping his fingers. A tiny flame erupted between his finger and thumb, flickering brightly.

Merrick curled a tentacle around his wrist, gently guiding him down to Ollie's chest. His tentacle glowed, and at first nothing was happening.

Chase concentrated, using all of his focus to keep the flame going. It was starting to burn his fingers, but he didn't stop.

Sloane's hands joined his, prismatic light erupting from his palms and healing the burn. "I've got you, Chase. Come on. Just hold on."

Loch's tentacles came next, and his wing curled protectively around his mate, glowing brightly. "And I've got you, my sweet Starkiller."

Chase couldn't take his eyes off the wound in Ollie's chest, whispering desperately, "Please. Fuckin' please. Please, please, please."

Please wake up. Please just fuckin' wake up!

The gash began to close.

Ollie still wasn't moving, but the wound left from the dagger was disappearing.

Even with Sloane's assistance, Chase's fingers were blistering. He refused to let the spell go, no matter how much it hurt, gritting his teeth as he focused all of his anger and grief into that tiny little flame. It glowed brighter and brighter, fueled by all the power surging around him, and it soon became blinding.

It had to be enough.

It just had to be.

"Uncle…." Ollie's voice was weak, but he was moving. His eyes were opening. "Uncle Elwood?"

"Ollie!" Chase let the flame go out and grabbed him, hugging him tight and gasping against his chest. "Fuck, kiddo, I thought I'd lost you! I thought you were gone!"

"Erg, I'm okay," Ollie coughed. He patted Chase's arm. "I'm okay. Can't breathe, just…." He paused and started screaming.

"What's wrong?" Chase looked up to see both Loch and Merrick leering down at them. "Right! Hey. Hey, hey, hey! It's okay! They're with me. Everything is totally fine! Okay? The one with the dead eyes is Merrick, and the snaky-neck one is Loch. He's Sloane's baby daddy."

Ollie whimpered and covered his eyes. "Okay, so none of that makes me feel any better. I'm just not gonna look. Nope, nope."

"Good to see you, Ollie," Sloane said cheerfully, rubbing his back. "Been a while."

"Yeah, I'm, uh…." Ollie squinted at Sloane's stomach. "Congratulations?"

"How did you know that would work?" Chase asked Merrick, touching his snout. "The lighter."

"I was not entirely sure it would." Merrick made a chuffing sound. "But we are in a world between worlds. I knew there was a chance that Oleander's soul would not have time to pass to Xenon yet. Souls are drawn there by the light of the bridge."

"We just had to make a bigger light to keep his soul back," Sloane finished with a happy smile. "It's like when we light candles on Dhankes."

"Exactly so," Merrick said. "The ignis vitae is a spark of life. A flame that comforts and calls to the human soul."

"Even when it's on its way out," Sloane added. "It's part of the ritual to create a ghoul, calling the soul back so it can be bound—"

"Yeah. So cool. So very cool. Can I go home now?" Ollie asked miserably. "I am o-fahfah-cially over all of this shit."

"We gotta make sure the coast is clear first," Chase said, helping Ollie sit up and giving him another hug. "Got everybody and their mom out there looking for you. Can't just pop up with you without an explanation."

"It could potentially cause mass panic," Loch chimed in, sounding very pleased with himself.

Sloane gave Loch's shoulder an affectionate pat. "That's right."

"Speaking of panic," Merrick griped, "I hope no one is upset, but Jeff Martin is gone."

"That son of a bitch!" Chase growled.

"Well, you were a little distracted making me less dead," Ollie reminded him, peeking through his fingers. "That Je-fahfah guy is a real prick."

Chase gritted his teeth. "Hey, Merry, can you track the portal that slimeball used to jump out of here?" He looked around the line of trees. "And hey, what the fuck happened to the rest of his asshole buddies?"

"They're gone as well." Merrick shook his head. "There were multiple portals. I do not know how, but the trails are too weak for us to follow." He bumped Chase's arm. "Worry not. Now we know he is using these worlds to hide and conspire his diabolical plans. We can start searching them all, one by one."

"You think he's gonna try again?" Sloane asked.

"Yeah," Chase confirmed. "There had to be at least thirty other Salgumel crazy people here. The fuckin' cult is bigger than we thought. And I'm sure it'll keep growing."

"What makes you so sure?"

"Well, they just got a giant eyeball of Merrick here wrecking their shit with that godly wrath of his. If any of them had doubts about the gods being real, we just made believers outta them."

"We may have unintentionally exacerbated the situation." Merrick bowed his head. "We may see an increase in Sagittarian fervor in the weeks to come."

Ollie raised his hand. "Look, Mr. Scary God Dude Merrick, I don't understand anything you're saying, but seriously, when can I go home?"

"We can return to Chase's residence and call off the search. We will tell them you were…." Merrick hesitated.

"Just tell them I was on a fuckin' bender."

"But that is not what happened."

"Doesn't matter what's true or not." Ollie shrugged sadly. "It's what they'll believe."

"That is… unfortunate."

"Life sucks," Ollie mumbled, tracing the place on his chest where the dagger had stabbed him. There was a thin line, almost silver in color, left behind. "But, uh, I'm glad I'm still around for it to suck. Or, you know, whatever. Thank you."

"Yeah, thank you, guys," Chase said, looking to Sloane and Loch. He took Sloane's hand to shake it. "For everything."

"Anytime," Sloane confirmed. "You have any more trouble with the cult, give us a call. I'll let you know if we hear anything on our end."

Merrick and Loch bumped their heads together, and their tails wrapped around one another's in what may have been a godly hug.

"Take care of your mate," Merrick was saying. "We shall have dinner with the frozen breadsticks soon."

"Yes," Loch agreed. "I wonder, did you finally act on your desires with your partner…?"

Merrick jerked back, cocking his head sheepishly. "Is that, is that really relevant right now?"

"Uncle!" Loch's wings flapped excitedly. "You *slut*!"

"That language is uncalled for!"

"But mortals use it ironically as a term of endearment!"

Sloane grinned. "Oh, well, I suppose more congratulations are in order, huh? Good for you, Chase."

Chase wanted to melt into the ground. "Yeah, thanks." He rubbed his blushing face. "It's great. It's really great. Now, time to go. Gotta get Ollie home, you know."

"Are you changing your name?" Loch asked curiously. "Gordoth the Touched doesn't quite have the same ring to it, eh?"

"We must attend to Oleander," Merrick huffed, ignoring the question. "I am expecting us all to remain vigilant from here on out. Though this attempt to raise Salgumel has failed, there will be more."

"We'll be ready," Sloane promised.

"Let's get goin'," Chase said, throwing his arm around Ollie's shoulders and reaching for Merrick. "Ready, kiddo?"

"So ready."

"Ah, one more thing," Merrick said, nodding at Chase. "Your hat?"

"Oh yeah." Chase frowned and looked around at the smoldering brush. "Damn thing has to be around here somewhere." He spotted a black blob and upon retrieval found it was the burned husk of his beloved fedora. "Well, shit."

"My dear mate, I'm so sorry." Merrick grimaced. "I know that hat was quite important to you."

"It's okay." Chase tried to wipe it off, and the burned felt crumbled in his hands. "I mean, it's not. It's fuckin' toast."

Merrick cleared his throat.

The hat was suddenly gone, and then it reappeared on top of Chase's head, fully restored. He had to take it off to look at it, and it looked just like it did the day he'd bought it two years ago. Coincidentally, that happened to be the same time he met Merrick. That thought made him smile, and he popped the hat back on his head.

It still didn't feel quite right, but hey, he'd take it.

Chase grinned, giving the hat a little tip as he said, "Okay. Now we're ready."

The search was ended, and Ollie corroborated their story that he'd gotten drunk, wrecked his place, and lost his way for a few days. Milo was the only other person who knew what had really happened. It hurt Chase to tell Ollie's parents that bogus crap, but Ollie was right.

They didn't question a thing.

After returning to Chase's apartment to retrieve Merrick's car, they drove Ollie home and walked him inside his apartment. Chase offered to stay to keep him company, but Ollie politely declined.

"I just wanna sleep," Ollie insisted. "For, like, a week. Maybe two."

"I'm sorry," Chase suddenly blurted out.

"For what?"

"You know…." Chase gestured vaguely. "You dying. Well, almost dying."

"You didn't stab me."

"But I got you mixed up in all this," Chase explained. "It's my fault they found out about you."

"Oh, right. I mean, well, that's okay. I mean, you didn't do it on purpose. And hey, we saved the world, right?" Ollie forced a smile. He looked so much older in that moment. "Guess a broken heart is good for something after all."

Chase pulled Ollie into a big hug. "I love you, kiddo."

"I love you too."

When they parted, Chase saw that Ollie's apartment had been magically cleaned up. There was no trace of the earlier invasion left now.

"I took the liberty of warding your residence," Merrick said from his spot hovering by the door. "You will be safe."

"Thanks," Ollie said, still hesitating to look directly at Merrick. "Don't suppose you can whip me up a pizza too?"

Merrick didn't seem to understand, but Chase quickly said, "Hey, I can order you up somethin'. Whatever you want." He frowned. "You sure you're okay bein' alone tonight?"

"I'm fine. I was kidding about the pizza. Kinda. I don't think I could eat anyway." Ollie ran his fingers through his hair. "I'm gonna go sleep. And sleep some more."

"You need anything at all, you call me, okay?"

"I will." Ollie headed off to his bedroom, but he paused. "Wait. There's something that Je-fahfah guy said. When they took me."

"What?"

"He was arguing with this other guy about looking for the first child of Azaethoth," Ollie replied. "Said they didn't need him now since the ritual was gonna work."

"The *first* child?" Merrick narrowed his eyes. "You are certain that is what he said?"

"Yeah. I mean, Great Azaethoth had twins, so I dunno what he was talking about." Ollie shrugged. "I thought maybe you guys might."

Chase saw Merrick's hand fidget, and he told Ollie, "Yeah, thanks, kiddo. We'll look into it. You get some sleep. Call me if you need me."

"Yeah, I will. Night, Uncle. Night, freaky god guy my uncle is dating."

Merrick didn't seem to like that title, but he replied, "Good night, Oleander. Sleep well."

Chase double-checked the locks before they left and then collapsed in the passenger seat of Merrick's car with a groan. He was exhausted.

Saving the world was fuckin' hard work.

Merrick got in behind the wheel and reached for his hand.

"Mmm, are we off duty?" Chase joked, turning his head to grin at him.

"Honestly, right now I could not even be bothered to care," Merrick said, shyly leaning in to kiss Chase's cheek. "It has been... a very interesting day."

"Who you tellin'? Fuck. I'm with Ollie. I think going to bed is a fantastic idea."

"I can leave you at home to rest if you would like—"

"No, no. I didn't mean I'd be going to bed alone." Chase rubbed his thumb over Merrick's knuckle. "I want you to stay with me again. Please."

"Oh!" Merrick smiled and ducked his head. "Yes, I believe that can be arranged. I would like that."

"Me too." Chase looked out the window as they drove away, his gaze lingering on Ollie's apartment.

There must have been something telling in his expression because Merrick asked him, "You are worried about Oleander?"

"Yeah." Chase grimaced. "Poor kid is seein' fuckin' crazy shit, gets his heart broken by the schmuck whose life he saved, and then he gets fuckin' stabbed. He ain't had it real good here lately."

"He is in great pain."

"You mean from the stabbing part or the broken heart part?"

"Both."

"Right." Chase looked down where their hands were still joined. "I wish… I wish I could go back to the night I arrested him. I wish I woulda believed him."

"But you believe him now. And you can offer him the support he so clearly needs."

"Still kinda feel like shit about it anyway." Chase grimaced. "And, uh, sorry about calling you a useless whatever-the-fuck."

"Forgiven, my mate." Merrick smirked. "If you feel so inclined, there are several ways you can apologize that may be satisfactory."

"Mmm, I'm definitely inclined." Chase fought back a yawn. His mind was on board, but his body was not cooperating. He fought to stay awake, asking, "So what's with this first child of Azaethoth? That's the Kindress thing, yeah?"

"Yes. The oldest of the gods say that Great Azaethoth's first child was a being of pure starlight who died before ever drawing its first breath," Merrick replied with a faint grimace. "In his grief, Great Azaethoth tried to bring the child back to life, but it became a monster. It was corrupted by his pain, his anguish, and soon it tried to destroy the universe."

"Well… fuck."

"To save all life as we know it, Great Azaethoth drowned the child in his own tears, for no other substance in creation can harm it. This began the never-ending cycle of the Kindress, a being that is cursed to live and die for all of eternity because Great Azaethoth cannot let him go."

"So wait, he kills his own kid, brings him back, and just kills him again?" Chase scoffed. "That is seriously fucked-up."

"This is why Great Azaethoth did not allow his other children or any of their descendants to have the power of resurrection," Merrick explained. "He feared that others would be trapped as he is, afraid to let their loved ones move on."

"Yeah, but most normal people's loved ones aren't gonna come back from the dead and try to destroy the universe."

"Which is why humans were allowed to learn the secrets of resurrection. As the very last of Great Azaethoth's children, you have the least amount of potential for epic destruction."

"Oh, goody. That was nice of him."

"You are very fragile compared to them. Sort of… squishy, if you will."

"Squishy?"

"The Asra, for example, can live for thousands of years. Humans, not so much. It makes sense why he allowed you the opportunity to cheat death when you are given so little life."

"You're so cheerful, you know that?"

Merrick narrowed his eyes suspiciously. "You are being sarcastic."

"Me?" Chase grinned. "Never."

"Hm…."

"So why would the cultists want to find this thing?"

"The Kindress is said to be a god of unimaginable power," Merrick replied. "I am confident they would attempt to harness that power and use it to wake Salgumel and help him destroy the world."

"Right. So, that's bad."

"Very."

"Good thing Great Azaethoth is always murdering him, yeah? Nothing to worry about."

"In theory." Merrick frowned. "The cultists should have come to the same conclusion, and yet they are still searching for it."

"Well, they're a bunch of crazy assholes. The fuck do they know?"

"I hope you are right."

Back at Chase's apartment, Merrick tidied up the abandoned mess of files from the case while Chase made coffee. Even though it wasn't very late, he was tired. He was also certain he had some mate-type duties to perform, and he didn't want to let Merrick down.

He was still dragging by the second cup, and his head was starting to hurt.

The case wasn't closed, not by far.

Sure, they had saved Ollie, but Jeff and the other cultists were still somewhere out there and had murder charges to answer for, on top of a whole litany of other crimes.

Then there was the question of the ritual; what if they found someone else with starsight or starlight magic and tried again? Who would be there to stop them?

And that starbaby thing, the Kindress. Why were they searching for something that just kept dying? How could they hope to find it?

"Time for sleep," Merrick ordered, walking over to him and prying the coffee cup out of his hands.

"But I'm not—" Chase was suddenly in bed, wearing nothing but his shorts, and Merrick was lying beside him. "Shit, that's still weird."

"My apologies."

"It's okay," Chase said, rolling over to kiss him. "Ain't put me off or nothin' like that. I'm still good to go."

"You are tired," Merrick replied, easing Chase back.

"So?" Chase was honestly too tired to fight and flopped over on his back.

"People do sleep in beds together without the risk of coitus, yes?" Merrick smirked, getting settled in the crook of Chase's shoulder.

"Well, yeah." Chase frowned. "I just figured, you know, you'd wanna…."

"Because we have had the one evening, you think I have become, what did Loch say, a slut?"

"No!" Chase's cheeks burned. "I just was making the offer! In case you wanted to!" He sighed. "I didn't want to disappoint you."

"I do not think you could if you tried," Merrick said, lifting his head for a kiss. His tentacles unraveled and wrapped around Chase's chest. "Mm, I know you need to rest. We will sleep tonight, and we can engage in physical relations in the morning… if you are lucky."

"Well," Chase mused, "I stopped a crazy guy from trying to end the world, resurrected my nephew, and got the god of my dreams here in my bed. Yeah, I'd say I'm pretty lucky."

"Yes, you are." Merrick fidgeted. "Although you did not technically resurrect him. You created a beacon that led his soul back to his body—"

"Merry?" Chase smiled fondly.

"Yes?"

"Love of my life, my godly mate?"

"Yes…?"

"Go to sleep."

"Good night." Merrick's tentacles curled around Chase a little tighter. "I love you."

"I love you too."

CHAPTER 15.

PHYSICAL RELATIONS were indeed enjoyed after a good night's sleep, and for the first time in his entire career, Detective Benjamin Merrick was late for work.

They enjoyed each other more responsibly after that, and Chase promised to set extra alarms every morning just in case.

The search for Jeff Martin and the other cultists remained intense, although no progress was made. Daisy disappeared before she could be questioned officially, doubtlessly reunited with her crazy buddies since her memory had been zapped. No one at the department was going to forget the cult's attempt to harm two of their own, and Chase wished he could tell them all the truth.

They knew exactly where ol' Jeffy boy was hiding out, but it just happened to be somewhere in a magical world that was one out of thousands, all of them forgotten by time....

Okay, "exactly" was a stretch.

Merrick and Loch searched the worlds known to them and their immediate family, and Sloane dug relentlessly through ancient texts and scrolls to find new ones with Ollie helping them translate. It made Chase feel a little useless, but he did what he could to support them, even if it was just making pasta and frozen breadsticks on demand.

Before Chase knew it, it had been two weeks since they'd stopped the ritual, and he and Merrick were having Sloane and Loch over for dinner.

Milo was also invited and brought his pregnant girlfriend, Lynnette Fields, who then told her brother, the real Lochlain Fields, and his husband, Robert, to come over too. Lochlain took it upon himself to invite his best friend, a ghoul named Fred Wilder, who came with his date, his doctor, a young man called Ell Sturm.

Well, Chase was glad he'd made plenty of food.

"We really do need T-shirts," Lynnette declared, leaning back in her chair at the small table and rubbing her little baby bump. "Some sort of Super Secret Sages' Club."

"I do not think that would be wise," Merrick grumbled.

"This is really everybody that knows, huh?" Chase called out from the kitchen, popping the breadsticks into the oven.

"Except for Ollie and Jay," Milo chimed in. He was standing behind Lynnette, rubbing her shoulders.

"Oh, and Alexander and Rota!" Sloane shouted back from where he was lounging on the couch with Loch. He didn't have the bump Lynnette did, but that didn't stop Loch from snuggling against his stomach and petting it reverently.

Chase stepped out of the kitchen. "And they are where exactly?"

"Off looking for the Fountain of the Kindress to find Rota's body."

"Right. The starbaby thing?"

"Yes," Merrick confirmed. "The Fountain is where Great Azaethoth gathers his tears to drown the child. I do not suppose you have any way to get in contact with Alexander or Rota?"

"Ugh, why would we?" Loch complained.

"If they have found a way to navigate the worlds between worlds, it would be very helpful as we continue our own search for the cultists," Merrick replied patiently.

"You still think they're hiding out there?" Sloane asked.

"Where else could they be?" Milo piped up. "Look, the entire AVPD has been tearing this city apart trying to find them. Either they've moved on or they're hunkered down at their very own porn temple."

"Unlikely," Loch said. "We checked all those."

"Worth mentioning that I've had an influx of requests for Sagittarian artifacts," Robert added, glancing warily between Chase and Merrick.

Robert, in addition to running a jewelry store, was also a fence and dealer in black market magical items.

Considering the combined criminal record of their guests was longer than Chase's arm, one of the first ground rules established for this little party was no arrests. Merrick was disappointed, but he'd promised to honor the agreement.

Even so, Robert seemed nervous.

"I'm talking by the dozens. More than I've ever had," he went on. "The buyers don't even care if they're broken or cursed, they just want them."

"I've also received several lucrative offers to relieve museums and private collectors of certain Sagittarian items," Lochlain said with a sly smile. "I've declined, of course."

"Of course," Merrick echoed.

Chase stepped out of the kitchen, eyeing Fred for a moment.

As a ghoul, his very existence was illegal, but Chase had to admit that he never would have clocked him. Fred was the freshest ghoul he'd ever seen. Didn't even smell bad.

Whatever that little Ell guy was doing, it was some good stuff.

Fred glared at him for staring, and Chase cleared his throat to address the room. "So, we got people out there wanting to buy up or steal all the Sage stuff that they can get their hands on, right?"

"Yup," Sloane replied. "There's even talk of an actual coven being formed."

"Some kind of spiritual resurgence?" Ell suggested quietly. "I mean, it could happen, right?"

"Buncha witches gettin' wise to the old ways all of a sudden seems mighty suspicious," Fred grumbled. "Someone is out there spreadin' the word."

"Our cult buddies, no fuckin' doubt," Chase agreed.

"I remember when I was a kid and being the only Sage I knew," Sloane said, taking Loch's hand in his. "If so many people are converting because that's what they feel is right in their hearts, great. I'm happy for them."

"But if they're only converting because they think the world is about to end and wanna be on the side doing the ending, not so great," Lynnette huffed.

"The AVPD is actively watching for any and all suspicious activity, especially Sagittarian," Merrick said. "While their intentions are noble, I am afraid that our people are not being held in a positive light."

"They think we're all crazy zealots?" Sloane asked knowingly.
"Yes."

"I mean, I only converted after Loch, His Holy Tentacleness, bopped me on the head with one of those bad boys," Milo protested, "but that doesn't make me crazy and wanna end the world."

"While that may be true for you, I suspect these new converts are being radicalized in anticipation of Salgumel's return," Merrick said grimly. "They are being prepared for a war."

"Let's not forget the recent pattern of my dear siblings doing their part to speed this little tiff along," Loch said, lifting his head from Sloane's lap. "And if Gronoch is to be believed, there are many other gods who support Salgumel's return."

"But hey!" Milo said cheerfully, pointing at Sloane. "We got our very own Starkiller, right? Crazy-ass mortals or gods, no problem!"

"Not even a Starkiller will mean much if they succeed in finding the Kindress," Merrick warned. "The firstborn child is a being made of pure starlight. A Starkiller's sword will be useless against it."

"You believe it's real, Uncle?" Loch frowned, a few of his tentacles unfurling to hold Sloane a little closer.

"Real enough to be concerned." Merrick raised his brow. "You forget, Nephew, I am one of the oldest of Baub's spawn. I was there when Abigail the Starkiller killed Halandrach and took Zunnerath as her mate. It is said she washed the blood off her hands there at the Fountain. If the Fountain is real, then so is the Kindress."

The timer on the oven dinged, and Chase scooted back into the kitchen to retrieve the breadsticks and plated out the pasta. All this talk of gods and blood was way over his head. Besides, with a pregnant lady out there, he wasn't gonna drag his feet on the grub.

Well, make that two pregnant people, one of whom was a man, two ancient gods, a ghoul, a ghoul doctor, a rogue witch, a criminal fence, and a Milo.

What a weird fuckin' family.

Family.

Huh.

The word surprised him and warmed his heart, and he suddenly recalled all the dinners he used to have with his brother before things went south. Maybe everyone here wasn't related by blood, but the collective desire to protect their world and all of humanity was good enough for Chase. He'd missed this more than he realized, and he liked having a full house to feed.

Other than worrying about what Loch was going to steal from him, it was great.

And, a little voice in the back of his head reminded him, also worrying about whether or not Ollie was okay.

After all, was it really a family gathering without his nephew here?

Ollie had declined the dinner invite. Chase didn't know if it was because of the godly company or a general aversion to seeing people, but he was concerned. As far as he knew, Ollie hadn't left the apartment since coming home from the ritual.

"There you go, worrying again," Merrick noted, his sudden presence in the kitchen startling Chase.

"Shit, you're sneaky!" Chase clutched his pounding heart. "Take it easy on me. I'm old."

"My apologies." Merrick kissed his cheek. "I came to check on you, and you have that look on your face."

"What look?"

"You are worried. Oleander?"

"Yeah. Kinda wish he woulda come." Chase held up his hands. "What can ya do, you know? He's miserable."

"Perhaps you should bring him some food?" Merrick suggested.

"Oh yeah, I guess we could…."

"No, just you." Merrick frowned. "He needs support, and I do not believe he finds my presence tolerable."

"Ah, that's just because he can see the real you all squished up in this body." Chase put his hand on Merrick's hip. "And for the record, the wings? Never did tell you how sexy I think they are…."

"Yes, you have."

"Mmm, did I also mention how hot your tentacles are?"

"Yes. You are trying to distract me from talking about your nephew with the promise of coitus."

"All this beauty and brains too." Chase kissed him sweetly.

"Your flattery will not deter me." Merrick held his head high. "Once our guests have departed, we are revisiting this conversation."

"The conversation about coitus, you mean? Well, fuck, come on! We got people to feed so we can get them all the hell out of here!"

Merrick sighed as if annoyed, but he couldn't stop smiling.

The conversation turned to more cheerful topics after Chase and Merrick passed out the plates. Everyone was excited for Sloane's Neun Monde celebration and the godly family that would be visiting. There was something about one of the goddesses being a mass of writhing tentacles, and Chase couldn't look at his spaghetti the same way again.

There was much discussion about baby names, and even Fred and Ell suggested a few. Milo and Lynnette were set on something inspired by some space show, and Sloane and Loch weren't sharing yet. Lochlain's suggestion was Lochlain, which everyone immediately turned down.

Just Lochlain and Loch were already confusing enough.

Fred and Ell were the first to leave, thanking Chase profusely for the meal even though Fred hadn't eaten a single bite. Lynnette had taken care of Fred's plate, but it wasn't sitting well on her pregnant belly, so she and Milo followed soon after, with Robert and Loch right behind them.

Sloane and Loch stayed long enough to help clean up before taking their leave, promising to send word if they found any new worlds where the cult might be hiding. Chase appreciated the offer, but it abruptly brought back the reality of their situation.

Jeff Martin was still out there with his cult, and their numbers were growing. Ancient gods were waking up, and not all of them were friendly—especially that Sally guy who had gone crazy and was gonna wreck the world if someone interrupted his nap.

At least the god Chase was in love with could be swayed by bad puns and frozen breadsticks.

Chase was putting the last of the dishes away, and he smiled when he felt Merrick's tentacles curl around his waist. "Mmm, yes?"

"I have been thinking." Merrick rested his chin on Chase's shoulder and hugged him from behind.

"About?" Chase grinned. "Oh, is this about the conversation about coitus?"

"No," Merrick said firmly.

"Hmmm."

"It is the one about Oleander. The one I said we were going to have after our guests departed."

"I know, I know." Chase dropped a hand on Merrick's forearm. "I was just thinking earlier that having everybody here? Having dinner like this? It was like having a really weird family reunion."

"Oh?"

"Except Ollie wasn't here." Chase smiled sadly. "I need to go see him. You're right."

"I do have that habit."

"Yeah, yeah, I know. He doesn't want help from me. Well, I'll make sure he gets it anyway. I'll check in on him tomorrow after work." Chase glanced back over his shoulder. "We, uh, staying at my place or yours?"

"Normally I would say you are being too presumptuous—" Merrick pursed his lips. "—but that is what I wanted to talk to you about."

"The, ahem, coitus?"

"No, I was thinking about whether or not we should reexamine our living situation."

"What do you mean?" Chase wiggled around in Merrick's tentacles to turn so they were facing each other.

"Being that we are mates and also partners, we spend a lot of time together," Merrick said, his jaw tight. "There have been many late nights together, more than not that we've spent in your bed or together in mine."

Chase studied Merrick's stern expression, and for once he couldn't get a read on where his head was at. "Yeah, and?"

"In an effort to be economically conscious and responsible regarding our fuel consumption, I was thinking… I would like…."

"What is it, Merr?"

"I would like to cohabitate with you," Merrick said finally, his stoic countenance faltering. "Please."

"Cohabi-what?" Chase grinned. "Wait. Are you asking me if I want us to move in together?"

"Yes. Maybe. Possibly." Merrick frowned. "Is that not an appropriate request? I can withdraw the offer—"

"No," Chase quickly replied. "I would love to cohabitate with you. Very much."

"Really?" Merrick's face lit up, his eyes turning black and shimmery.

"Really." Chase pressed their lips together, and he sighed as Merrick's tentacles coiled around him.

Merrick kissed him back passionately, his hands and slithering appendages slipping beneath Chase's shirt.

Chase groaned, his skin prickling with heat. He held on to Merrick's hips and pulled him close. "Mmm, I guess this means you wanna have dessert in the bedroom, eh?"

"Dessert?" Merrick paused. "But you did not make anything…."

Chase waited.

"Ah, you mean the coitus. The coitus is dessert."

"Yes, the coitus." Chase's snickers were soon lost in Merrick's lips. He didn't notice the change in position as Merrick magically whisked them away until he opened his eyes to see his bedroom ceiling above him.

"My mate," Merrick murmured, gazing down at Chase as their clothes melted away. "I long to wake up every day with you, to take you to bed every night just like this…."

"I'm totally fuckin' down." Chase kissed him, groaning low as he felt his body slowly stretch in preparation for Merrick's tentacles.

"I thought you might be."

"Can we, like…." Chase paused, trying to quickly figure out the logistics of what he wanted to do. "Can you get on your back?"

"Why?"

"So I can ride that big ol' tentadick."

Merrick's mouth opened and closed, and then he nodded. "I believe I can accommodate your request."

"Thought so." Chase laughed as Merrick quickly changed their positions and pulled him on top. Chase adjusted himself, straddling Merrick's hips and bracing his hands on his chest. "Yeah? Like this?"

"Yes." Merrick slid his hands up Chase's thick thighs. "Definitely like this."

Chase groaned when he felt one of Merrick's tentacle-dicks pressing between his legs. He eased himself back, letting his weight bring him down on the tip. "Ahhh... fuck...."

"Mm, Elwood," Merrick whispered, gazing up at him reverently. "You look so beautiful like this. Is it, is it too much? Do I need to move...?"

"Uh-uh," Chase replied, sitting down a little more and making himself moan. "Just keep it right there, right there. Mmm, I've got this."

"Yes, my mate."

Rolling his hips, Chase worked more of Merrick's massive tentacle-cock inside of him. He could feel how wet he was thanks to Merrick's magic, and his ass was stretching out to take it all. It wasn't pain, not exactly, but it was a sensation of pressure, hot and slick, and he wanted more.

He sat back, his fingers dragging down Merrick's stomach as he felt the knot pushing against his hole. He took a few quick breaths and began to grind, his head tipping back with a greedy groan. "Ohhhh, fuck.... Merry...."

The knot was right there, and Chase's hole was already so tight. A brief flicker of pain made his movements falter, and his breathing hitched as he tipped forward. Fuck, he was so close.

"Mm, Elwood," Merrick gasped, his hands moving up Chase's body, groping his broad shoulders. "You feel so wonderful. You always feel so very good."

"I've got you, baby boy," Chase promised, whipping his hair out of his face. "You just wait. You ain't seen shit yet." He gritted his teeth and slammed his hips down, crying out as the knot finally popped inside.

"Elwood!" Merrick's entire body jerked, and his tentacles spiraled around Chase's legs.

"Oh *fuck* yeah." Chase grinned, his mouth hanging open as he got his hips rolling, thrusting down on Merrick's thick tentacle-cock. His entire body felt like it was glowing, shimmering with bliss, and he gave all he had to the god beneath him.

He clawed at Merrick's hips, riding him hard and dropping down to take all of him over and over again. He was so full, and Merrick's tentacle was stroking intimate nerves deep within him that he didn't even know he had. This angle was creating the most delicious sensation, and his skin was buzzing all over.

The continued pressure sent an electric shiver up his spine, and his nipples were getting hard in its wake. Every hair was standing on end, and the slide of Merrick's tentacle was making him ache. The knot was plunging deeper inside of him, and he didn't know how much more he could—

"Ah, fuck!" Chase cried out as he came, watching his cock shoot across Merrick's stomach, pulsing with every slam. His legs were giving out, trembling violently, but he didn't want it to stop.

Merrick was there to take over, his powerful tentacles wrapping all around him and lifting him up so he could keep thrusting. He caressed Chase's aching thighs, praising, "You feel so perfect, you are always so perfect... I love you, I love you so much, Elwood."

"Love you too," Chase panted in reply, his body twitching when Merrick came inside of him. His own climax was still going, and the hot rush of come inside of him made it sweeter still.

Right as the bliss was beginning to ebb, Merrick was stuffing his other tentacle-dick in Chase's hole. All Chase could do was sob from the sudden way his body was forced to open up, and he groaned as a second load flooded his body.

He could actually feel Merrick lifting him right off the bed from the force of his thrusts, and he tipped forward to bury his face down in Merrick's chest. Both tentacles were wiggling and thrusting, and Chase couldn't stop screaming in pleasure. "Oh yes, Merry... oh fuck, fuck, yes... oh, *fuck me!*"

His climax never stopped, one wave of pleasure rolling into the next without pause, and Chase's heart was about to explode right out of his chest. The swell of both fat knots inside of him was teetering on pain, and he fought to breathe through the inescapable pressure.

It was so damn good, so fucking good, and Chase whimpered as one final orgasmic shudder ran through his body. The tentacle-cocks were pulling out with the utmost care, and a gush of come dripped between Chase's legs.

Fingers tingling, he reached back to feel, finding his hole open and wet. His body was already trying to clench back up, and he let out a quiet moan when Merrick's fingers joined his own.

"I love this," Merrick crooned, kissing Chase's hair. "I love knowing what I do to you."

"You fuckin' wreck me, every time. Fuck." Chase tried to laugh, but he was too out of breath. "That was good."

"Did I hurt you?"

"No, baby, I'm fine." Chase went limp against Merrick's chest. "Just, you know, got fucked by a god, and now none of my muscles wanna function."

Stroking Chase's back, Merrick sighed happily. "Well, you did most of the work this time. I liked that. Very much."

"Oh, we're definitely doing that again." Chase lifted his head for a quick smooch. "Mmm, at least twice a week."

"Oh, is that so?"

"Uh-huh." Chase beamed. "I mean, I got to ride you as a dragon, but this is way more fun."

"I love you." Merrick ran his fingers through Chase's hair. "Mm, you are absolutely perverted, and I love you very much."

"Hey, not many people get to say they corrupted a god. I'm pretty proud, you know."

"As you should be," Merrick confirmed. He wordlessly cleaned up the mess and refreshed the sheets, but he kept Chase on top of him. "I am looking forward to an eternity of your particular brand of corruption."

"You know I don't exactly have that kinda time." Chase smirked. "But I'm glad to spend what I got with you."

"Oh, do not be ridiculous," Merrick scoffed. "You are my mate. When you are ready, we will ascend to Zebulon together, and you will be reborn as a god by my side."

"Really?" Chase perked up. "You'd do that for me?"

"Of course. I love you."

"I love you too, Merr." Chase wagged his brow. "So, can we do that whole ascension bein' a god thing now?"

"No, not yet."

"Lemme guess, there's some rules?"

"Your mortal life here is not yet exhausted. I do not want to waste it."

"Yeah, but being a god would be really cool…."

"If we were to ascend now, we would most likely fall into the dreaming with the other gods. Which, while very peaceful, does not involve any coitus."

"Okay." Chase laughed. "I've changed my mind."

A phone rang, and the tune identified it as the new one Merrick had purchased last week.

Merrick opened his hand, and the phone simply appeared. He cleared his throat, answering it politely, "Detective Merrick here."

Chase was close enough to hear the person calling, and it was Milo.

"Hey!" Milo greeted. "Sorry to call so late, but I wanted to give you a heads-up. A Super Secret Sage Club kind of heads-up?"

"We are listening. What is wrong?"

"I just got called in for a crime scene. One of our would-be cultists just got himself a big ol' case of dead-itis."

"Was it Jeffrey Martin?" Merrick's eyes widened.

"Nope, sorry. It's one of the other guys who shot at you over at the shoe factory. Name is Clyde Wynette."

"Where?"

"The alley behind the always classy and chic Dead to Rites."

"Why us? We are not homicide."

"Bartender says he met up with some guys at the bar, they all had some drinks, then he stumbled outside into the alley for some relief because using a bathroom isn't cool enough, and, uh, that's where he drowned."

"Wait," Chase piped up, "so this guy drowned in the middle of a back alley?"

"Yup," Milo confirmed. "Oh, it gets better. It was salt water. Salinity confirms that it's seawater. Like, from the ocean."

"The fucking fuck."

"That's why magic enforcement is being called."

"We shall be awaiting the call from dispatch," Merrick said grimly.

"You guys have a great night!" Milo exclaimed. "Probably see you soon!"

"Goodbye, Milo."

"This sounds like a shitty riddle," Chase complained once Merrick hung up. "How the hell do you drown in the ocean when there's no damn ocean?"

"We should get dressed," Merrick said. "We may very well have to visit the crime scene tonight."

"Mm. Can't wait." Chase groaned loudly when Merrick's phone began to ring again. "Ah, come on. Wanted to at least get some more cuddles in."

"That will be dispatch." Merrick swept them out of bed and had them dressed in a blink. He stood up straight, pausing to adjust Chase's hat. "Ready to go, partner?"

"For you?" Chase winked. "Always."

K.L. HIERS is an embalmer, restorative artist, and queer writer. She has been writing for over twenty years, penning her very first book at just eight years old. Publishers generally do not accept manuscripts in Hello Kitty notebooks, however, but she never gave up.

She now enjoys writing professionally, focusing on spinning tales of sultry passion, exotic worlds, and emotional journeys. She lives in Zebulon, NC, with her husband and their children, some of whom have paws and a few who only pretend to because they think it's cute.

Website: http://www.klhiers.com

A SUCKER FOR LOVE MYSTERY

ACSQUIDENTALLY IN LOVE

K.L. HIERS

"A breezy and sensual LGBTQ paranormal romance."
—*Library Journal*

A Sucker For Love Mystery

Nothing brings two men—or one man and an ancient god—together like revenge.

Private investigator Sloane sacrificed his career in law enforcement in pursuit of his parents' murderer. Like them, he is a follower of long-forgotten gods, practicing their magic and offering them his prayers… not that he's ever gotten a response.

Until now.

Azaethoth the Lesser might be the patron of thieves and tricksters, but he takes care of his followers. He's come to earth to avenge the killing of one of his favorites, and maybe charm the pants off the cute detective Fate has placed in his path. If he has his way, they'll do much more than bring a killer to justice. In fact, he's sure he's found the man he'll spend his immortal life with.

Sloane's resolve is crumbling under Azaethoth's surprising sweetness, and the tentacles he sometimes glimpses escaping the god's mortal form set his imagination alight. But their investigation gets stranger and deadlier with every turn. To survive, they'll need a little faith… and a lot of mystical firepower.

www.dreampsinnerpress.com

A SUCKER FOR LOVE MYSTERY

Kraken My
Heart

K.L. HIERS

A Sucker For Love Mystery

It's just Ted's luck that he meets the love of his life while covered in the blood of a murder victim.

Funeral worker Ted Sturm has a foul mouth, a big heart, and a knack for communicating with the dead. Unfortunately the dead don't make very good friends, and Ted's only living pal, his roommate, just rescued a strange cat who's determined to make his life even more miserable. This cat is more than he seems, and soon Ted finds himself in an alternate dimension... and on top of a dead body.

When Ted is accused of murder, his only ally in a strange world full of powerful magical beings calling for his head is King Grell, a sarcastic, randy, catlike immortal with impressive abilities... and anatomy. The two soon find themselves at the center of a cosmic conspiracy and surrounded by dangerous enemies. But with Ted's special skills and Grell's magic, they have a chance to get to the bottom of the mystery and save Ted. There's just one problem: Ted's got to resist Grell's aggressive advances... and he isn't sure he wants to.

www.dreamspinnerpress.com

A SUCKER FOR LOVE MYSTERY

Head Over
Tentacles

K.L. HIERS

A Sucker For Love Mystery

Private investigator Sloane Beaumont should be enjoying his recent engagement to eldritch god Azaethoth the Lesser, AKA Loch. Unfortunately, he doesn't have time for a pre-honeymoon period.

The trouble starts with a deceptively simple missing persons case. That leads to the discovery of mass kidnappings, nefarious secret experiments, and the revelation that another ancient god is trying to bring about the end of the world by twisting humans into an evil army.

Just another day at the office.

Sloane does his best to juggle wedding planning, stopping his fiancé from turning the mailman inside out, and meeting his future godly in-laws while working the case, but they're also being hunted by a strange young man with incredible abilities. With the wedding date looming closer, Sloane and Loch must combine their powers to discover the truth—because it's not just their own happy-ever-after at stake, but the fate of the world....

www.dreamspinnerpress.com